"I want to se[e]
Brett wh[...]

"I don't think—"

"I never got a real date. It wasn't very nice to cancel that way."

Tricia shook her head. "I'm sorry, but—"

"Good, then I'll accept your apology Friday night when we go out. Think you can get a sitter?"

When Tricia hesitated, Brett pressed his advantage. "Because if you can't, I can probably call your friend Charity to sit for you. But then I'd have to explain how you canceled out on the first date and—"

"I can get one." And with that, she left with her kids.

He should have been counting his blessings that her son had tried to stop all this craziness before any real damage was done. But he could only feel relieved and grateful he'd get the chance to see Tricia again.

Books by Dana Corbit

Love Inspired

A Blessed Life #188
An Honest Life #233
A New Life #274

DANA CORBIT

has been fascinated with words since third grade, when she began stringing together stanzas of rhyme. That interest, and an inherent nosiness, led her to a career as a newspaper reporter and editor. After earning state and national recognition in journalism, she traded her career for stay-at-home motherhood.

But the need for creative expression followed her home, and later, through the move from Indiana to Michigan. Outside the office, Dana discovered the joy of writing fiction. In stolen hours, during naps and between carpooling and church activities, she escapes into her private world, telling stories from her heart.

Dana makes her home in Michigan, with her husband, three young daughters and two cats.

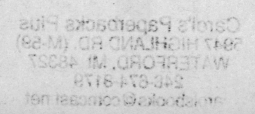

A NEW LIFE

DANA CORBIT

Steeple
Hill®

Published by Steeple Hill Books™

STEEPLE HILL BOOKS

**Steeple
Hill**®

ISBN 0-373-87284-4

A NEW LIFE

www.SteepleHill.com

Printed in U.S.A.

But they that wait upon the Lord shall renew their strength; they shall mount up with wings as eagles; they shall run, and not be weary; and they shall walk, and not faint.

—*Isaiah* 40:31

To my parents, James and Janet Corbit and Curt and Alice Berry. Thank you for being convinced for me even when I wasn't sure and for listening to my stories, each more fanciful than the last.

I would like to wish a special thanks to Lieutenant Joel Allen, Trooper Christopher Grace and Trooper Rene Gonzalez of the Michigan State Police for opening their world to me. Any mistakes in the story are my own.

Chapter One

"Strike. Yes!"

Max shot both hands into the air and did a happy dance on the lane, though two pins—the four and the nine—still stood firmly.

"Oh, brother," six-year-old Rusty, Jr. said, shaking his head. "They call that a 'split,' not a 'strike.'"

Max shrugged, showing off his million-dollar grin. "Split. Yes," he called out, repeating the dance with the gusto of a four-year-old.

Tricia Williams laughed out loud, and her three children fell into a cackling heap on top of their spring jackets that were piled on the floor. Their squeals only added to the noisy Saturday night atmosphere at Milford Bowling Lanes, combining with the crash of pins and the loud music from a nearby private event room.

It felt great to laugh again, to really laugh and not to feel as if she had to push air from her diaphragm to bolster the sound. In the two years since her husband Rusty's death, she'd sensed a compassionate—but relentless—scrutiny from her friends at Hickory Ridge Community Church who wanted to make sure she was all right. And she was. Her children were, too. Maybe her little family wasn't back to normal, but they'd found a new normal. If only she could convince her friends that she was fine.

"Hey, sweet pea, why don't you roll your ball again and see if you can hit one of those pins?" she told Max as she extracted him from the pile.

With another between-the-legs, agonizingly slow roll, the boy picked up the four pin, assisted by a good bounce from the gutter guards.

While the young mother marked down the score, her daughter Lani leaned close to whisper in her ear. "Do you think we should tell the man on the next lane that they can put the gutter things up for him, too?"

The struggle not to laugh again made Tricia's chest ache. She'd been trying not to notice the dark-haired man on lane fourteen for the last twenty minutes, since he'd settled in and started throwing a record-setting number of gutter balls. He was either terribly distracted or the worst bowler she'd ever seen.

"No, we'd better not," Tricia whispered back, giving her daughter a side glance. Lani's sly smile showed she was joking and, as always, she seemed older than her seven years. Tricia reached up to ruffle the deep-brown tresses of her child's bob haircut.

"Mom, watch me bowl." Rusty, Jr. stood poised with an eight-pound ball, wiggling his backside into his best pro bowling form.

"Okay, let's see you roll a strike. You're doing it just right."

It felt right, too, just being here on a rare night out with her three favorite people, even if it strained the tightrope budget she tried so hard to balance every month. Watching her children enjoy themselves almost relieved her guilt over telling the white lie that freed up her calendar for a bowling night. Almost, but not quite.

They continued through the frames of their game, but none of their performances compared to the show going on in the next lane. While before, the man couldn't hit a pin with a two-by-four, now his black ball seemed unable to miss one. Tricia half expected someone to recognize him at any moment as an escapee from the pro-bowlers' tour.

"Look, Mommy, the man isn't throwing gutter balls anymore," Max pointed out two octaves louder than his regular speaking voice.

Tricia pressed an index finger to her lips to hush her son, her cheeks burning. At least the guy had the decency not to look at them, though he must have heard. His chest moved slightly a few times as he seemed to be trying not to laugh. His profile transformed as a dimple, incongruous with the earlier determined flex of his jaw, appeared on his cheek. On his next frame, he even missed a pin.

"Kids, what are we here to do? Bowl or talk?"
Tricia said finally.

"Bowl!" the three chorused as they turned back
from their interesting neighbor.

So they returned to the game, with Tricia's applause
and encouragement accompanying her children's giggles. But no matter how hard she tried to focus on the
game, she couldn't help sneaking curious glances at
the next lane.

Why was such a handsome man bowling alone on
a Saturday night? Why had he seemed so preoccupied
when he'd arrived? And an even bigger question: why
did it matter to her? He was probably just like the four
of them, trying to get one last visit in before the bowling alley closed so it could be renovated into a mini-
mall. Besides, she hadn't been so much as curious
about a member of the male gender in the last two
years.

No one would know it from the number of blind
dates she'd gone on recently. It seemed that everyone
with a Christian friend-of-a-friend had introduced
them, hoping to create a perfect match. Her friend
Charity probably had the same hopes for the blind date
Tricia was supposed to have been on tonight. If she
hadn't cancelled.

Didn't these matchmakers realize she was already
in love—with Rusty. And she always would be. He'd
just gone to be with God a little ahead of her, that was
all. She couldn't blame her well-meaning church
friends; they just didn't understand. God only gave

people one love like that in a lifetime, and she'd already had hers. Even though she was a widow and only twenty-six, she didn't think it was fair of her to ask Him for more.

Trying to focus, Tricia rolled her ball. She smiled at her children over her dismal effort but suddenly felt too guilty to laugh with them. It wasn't her blind date's fault that her heart was permanently off the market. She'd been rude to cancel at the last minute. Tomorrow, right after church, she would phone him and try to reschedule.

Obviously, she needed to stop being nosy about the man in the next lane and focus on her own behavior. Still, out of her peripheral vision, she watched the man as he stepped off the lane and sipped his soda. He swiped his hand through his dark-brown hair, but since it was clipped so close, it did little more than flutter. Funny how the haircut made his strong jaw appear so pronounced.

"My turn now," Max called out, grabbing his ball and rushing up to throw it.

It might have been his best effort yet if he'd bowled in the right lane, instead of the one being used by their distracted neighbor.

"Wait, Max," Lani called out too late.

Max's eyes were wide as he turned to look back at the man. Tricia choked back a laugh. Maybe it was time to turn in those glamorous bowling shoes. But she'd paid good money for this game, and she wasn't about to leave until they'd bowled their last frame.

Prepared to apologize for her child, she turned toward the guy she'd been trying to ignore all night. A pair of startling light-brown eyes looked down at her before the guy threw back his head and laughed.

Brett Lancaster couldn't believe he was laughing. Especially at the woman staring back at him. Or about any female after the day he'd had—the last few *years* he'd had. But then she laughed along with him, her children joining her like a merry pack of hyenas.

Before, he'd noticed how striking the woman was. Only a blind man would have missed that. But when a smile spread across her heart-shaped face, she transformed into movie-star dazzling. With the contrast of that shiny, dark hair and fair, flawless skin, she resembled a porcelain doll, one that had just been removed from the box for a trip to…the bowling alley.

The crash of pins from that slow-moving ball stirred him from his reverie in time to remember his manners and stop staring. He turned to see the pins, in real-time slow motion, fall one by one.

"Wow, sport, you got a strike." Brett stepped forward and extended his hand for a high-five. The boy looked to his mother for approval before giving a slap that smarted.

"Sorry." Twin pink spots stained the woman's cheeks. "Max accidentally bowled on the wrong lane."

"Why are you apologizing? Young Max here just

improved my score. Thanks, kiddo. You know, I wasn't doing so well earlier.''

''Yeah, you needed some of these gutter things like we have,'' the older boy chimed. ''If you ask at the desk—''

''Thanks, but I don't need them now. My score's getting pretty good.''

''Because I got a strike,'' Max announced importantly.

''I'm doing really good, too.'' The older boy pulled the sheet off the scoring table and flashed it at him.

''Why aren't you keeping score?'' asked the girl who looked like a junior version of her mother.

''I didn't figure I'd win any trophies.''

He couldn't help smiling at the endearing way the children angled for his attention, perhaps as they would when their dad came home from work. Did he come home? Discreetly, he glanced at the mother's left hand. She wore no wedding ring, or any other rings for that matter.

An unsettling sensation moved inside his chest, something he attributed to indignation on this family's behalf. These sweet kids were probably victims of another deadbeat dad, like so many of the troubled youths he dealt with in his work. The guy had probably walked out on this young mother after promising her the world.

The woman caught him staring and blushed even more prettily, fidgeting with her delicate hands. ''Come on, guys, we've bugged the gentleman for long enough.'' She glanced at her watch. "We need to finish this game and get home. It's getting late, and we have church in the morning.''

"Aw, Mom," came the trio in chorus.

"Please, just one more game?" the girl said.

Brett was glad the child hadn't turned that cajoling tone on him, or he might have given her his car and thrown in a twenty-CD changer for good measure. A bad idea since he was driving a loaner from his dad's dealership tonight.

Not taking time to wonder why he wanted to spend even more of his Saturday night in a bowling alley with a mom and her passel of children, he approached the taller of the two petite brunettes.

"Come on, Mom," he said, using the same tone the girl had used. "Just one more game. You won't get the chance after this place closes.''

The way "no" was written in her stiff posture made him glad he hadn't offered to spring for the game. She probably thought he was an ax murderer who bowled while his ax was being sharpened. He'd already turned to retrieve his badge from the bi-fold wallet in his jacket pocket when she finally spoke.

"That's probably not a good idea—"

"I'm not a criminal, really." Maybe not a criminal, but desperate—he sure sounded that. To cover the awkward silence, he extended his hand and said, "I'm Brett Lancaster.''

He would have continued by saying "Michigan State Police," the way he usually did, but this lady blanched at his name alone. Now that was a reaction he'd never received from a woman.

Unable to resist a call to protect, he reached beneath her elbow to steady her. Her skin was so smooth where she'd pushed up her shirt sleeve, he could have sworn he'd grasped fine silk. He almost worried he'd snag it with his own calloused palm.

"Is there something I can get for you, ma'am? Water?"

She shook her head, but she still appeared dazed. The children weren't any help, crowding their mother and making worried sounds instead of giving her room to breathe.

Finally, when he couldn't decide whether to shake her alert or call for a paramedic, she offered a strange, apologetic smile and extended her free hand. "Hi, I'm Tricia Williams. And these are my children Lani, Rusty, Jr. and Max. Kids, this is Mr. Lancaster."

Tricia Williams? His frustration from earlier began to fester again but the feeling subsided. This was too funny to make him mad. Who ever heard of getting stood up and then ending up meeting face-to-face out on the town, anyway?

Coincidence? Not really. The village of Milford, Michigan, was too small for any chance meeting to be called a coincidence. There just weren't that many places to go. And since he hadn't called in to pick up his messages—and her cancellation—until he was already on Milford Road just outside the village limits, he'd figured the bowling alley was as good a place as any to blow off some steam. He deserved at least that after being idiot enough to let his sister badger him into a blind date in the first place. Had he learned nothing from his last relationship fiasco? Like never to get involved again?

"Tricia. So we finally meet." Brett chuckled as he reached to shake her hand, but his laughter died as soon as they touched. Her hand felt so small, while his was huge and clumsy. As their gazes connected, he glimpsed sadness beneath her smile, but Tricia glanced at the ground and pulled her hand away. When she looked up at him again, whatever he'd seen before had disappeared.

"Yes, finally. Charity has been trying to arrange this thing forever."

"Oh, yeah, Charity, my sister Jenny's friend from the hospital. So that's how this whole thing got set up."

Now that he knew her identity, he also remembered the vague details his matchmaker sister had provided: attractive, Christian, age twenty-six, widowed mother of three. That last detail had nearly made him call the whole thing off, but his sister's persuasive skills were legendary. Before, he'd suspected that this woman had been deserted, but now that he knew who she was, he also understood Tricia had been forsaken in a more painful and permanent way.

"Mommy, look at this," Lani called out.

They turned to see the children taking turns leaning over the ball return, the fan blowing their hair.

"Okay, guys, we'll finish this game and play another quick one. Then it's home to baths and bed."

Squeals of delight caused others at nearby lanes to shoot curious glances their way.

But Max drew his eyebrows together. "No bath."

His mother whisked him up in her arms and started spinning. "Yes, bath. With lots and lots of soap."

The child made a face only a mother could love and scrambled out of her arms. Rusty, Jr. was already winding up for his frame, while his sister sat at the desk, attempting to keep score. Happiness lit Tricia's eyes as she turned back to Brett.

"So this is what you cancelled on me for?" he couldn't help asking. Tricia's shoulders shifted. "Your exact words on my machine were 'I'm sorry, but something important came up.'"

She nodded. "And something important did. Actually, three important things."

"I can see that." He could. So why did he feel strangely jealous over the children she had chosen to spend time with rather than him? He should have been used to having women toss him away by now.

"I tried to reach you before you left home. Charity told me you rent a house in Brighton."

"I do, but I had some errands to run and came into town early."

She didn't ask him to elaborate, which was just as well because he would like to forget about his visit to his parents' house in Bloomfield Hills and the disappointment he still sensed every time his dad looked at him. When would his family finally accept that he was doing something for himself this time and they weren't going to change his mind? On the next lane over, he watched several pins fall, except for a lonely six pin. He, too, was standing alone these days. It wasn't the life he'd expected, but at least he'd regained his pride by following his heart.

Surprised he'd been daydreaming again, Brett glanced back at Tricia and caught her studying him. Though she looked away, a sensation of warmth settled in his chest.

"Well, I'm up pretty soon, so…"

He should have appreciated her attempt to make it easy for him to bow out, but he found he wasn't ready to leave. Instead of answering her, he crossed the hardwood surface to where her little girl was preparing to bowl.

"You know, Lani, I bet you'd hit more pins if you tried this." He pointed to the arrows on the floor. "Try aiming your ball at the very center arrow."

Soon, he had all three children vying for his bowling tips and the grown-up attention from "Mr. Brett" that went with them. No way would he admit it to his fellow troopers at the Brighton Post, but this had to count as his best Saturday night in months. No, he wouldn't allow his thoughts to go there and spoil the happy moment.

In the middle of an arms-looped celebration dance with Rusty, Jr. over the boy's first strike, Brett caught sight of Tricia watching him again, her expression stark without the contented mask she'd worn all night.

How he could have missed her lovely eyes before, he couldn't imagine. Framed by spiky lashes, they were dark, shiny brown and huge, strangely both too large for her face and perfect in their porcelain backdrop. Their hollow quality, though, captured him, reeling him in, making him ache in the vicinity of his heart. She looked like a waif, and he felt this need to protect her. For an unguarded second, her expression hinted she just might let him.

Brett wasn't sure what had passed between him and the mother of the Williams children—only that whatever it was, Rusty, Jr. had seen it, too. With an abrupt jerk, the boy ripped away his hand and marched to the bench, where he dumped off his bowling shoes.

"Mom, it's time to go. We have to get up for church." Already, the boy had his sneakers on and was holding up Max's for him.

It didn't take a psychology degree for Brett to recognize the boy's jealousy over his mother. He couldn't blame him for feeling threatened. What had he been thinking, looking at Tricia with the hope that he could heal her heart, that maybe she could even heal his?

"He's right. We'd better get home." Tricia's gaze was apologetic, if guarded. Had she felt it, too?

Max stomped his foot. "I don't want to go."

"But we're having fun," Lani whined. "Do we have to?"

"It's getting late. I'll have to drag you guys out of bed in the morning."

Tricia bent to change her shoes, but Max wouldn't budge. He sat down cross-legged on the floor and folded his arms.

"Max, do I need to count to three?" Tricia asked in a low warning, but the boy didn't even look up. "One…two—"

Before she could reach three, Brett scooped him up and tickled his belly. "Hey, bud, you'd better listen to your mom. You don't want her to say we can't play together anymore, do you?" Upside down, Max shook his head.

Tricia's surprised expression showed she'd gotten the message about another play date. As he carried the child to her, she met him halfway, probably to remain out of her older son's earshot.

"I want to see you again," Brett whispered.

She accepted Max into her arms. "I don't think—"

"I never got a real date. It wasn't very nice to cancel that way. Not quite a lie, but almost."

She shook her head. "I'm sorry, but—"

"Good, then I'll accept your apology Friday when we go out." As he waited for her to look at him, he sensed victory. "Think you can get a sitter?"

When she hesitated, he pressed his advantage. "Because if you can't, I can probably call your friend, Charity. But then I'd have to explain how you cancelled out on the first date and—"

"I can get one."

With that she stalked away and helped Max tie his shoes. Rusty, Jr. refused to look in Brett's direction, but Lani kept peeking back. Both she and Max waved at him as their mother hurried them out the door.

The bowling alley felt empty as soon as the troop left. If he had any sense at all, Brett would simply forget to call about Friday and chalk the whole situation up to bad judgment in his letting Jenny set him up. He was in way over his head by considering even one real date with a widow, let alone a widow with children. If Tricia Williams's baggage was weighed at an airport, it would be stamped "heavy" and slapped with a surcharge. But here he was tempted to offer to carry it for her, anyway.

He should have been counting his blessings that her son had tried to stop all this craziness before any real damage was done. But he could only feel relieved and grateful he'd get the chance to see Tricia again.

Chapter Two

A digital bedside clock and a distant street lamp offered the only illumination as Tricia collapsed, fully clothed, onto her bed an hour later, the bed-and-bath routine behind her. From the way her body ached, she would have guessed it was past midnight, but the red clock numbers confirmed it was only nine-thirty. As shadow and light slow-danced along the wall in the shape of maple tree branches, she wondered how long it had been since she'd slept. Truly slept. Days had become months and then metamorphosed into years when she wasn't watching.

She couldn't shake the image of Rusty, Jr., who had radiated tension as she'd helped him out of the shower and into his pajamas. His misplaced fury was transferred to everything around him, from the comb that wouldn't go through his hair to the stuffed dog that landed on the floor next to his bed. He had every right to his anger, for all he'd lost. She understood it, felt it down to her soul.

Nervous tension had her scooting across the bed to flip on the lamp, letting the warm yellow light bathe what had become her favorite room. Here she could be alone with her memories of Rusty, warm thoughts of his arms around her and private thoughts of the sweet intimacies of their marriage.

Reaching for her wedding band on the table and slipping it on, she surveyed the room. In the far corner, she could still see Max's cradle where it once had rested. A smile settled on her lips as she envisioned her family's first day in the house, her belly still swollen with the promise of their youngest child. Rusty and she had tumbled together on the bed that night, too exhausted from moving furniture to even love each other in the bungalow they'd struggled to finally afford.

She'd felt so safe then—and always—in his arms. The way she never did now. The way she never would again.

Memories of her husband flashed in her thoughts, in brilliant color this time when they'd become more like a sepia photograph lately, in danger of crumbling. But why were the memories coming tonight, when she needed rest to prepare her for the ordeal of going to church?

The Sunday tradition of attending services as a family was once the highlight of her week, even if they were continually late, and someone was always whispering or making paper airplanes with the bulletins. They were together then, worshiping God. The way it should be. Now every time she sat listening to one of Reverend Bob Woods's sermons, something seemed missing. Not her belief. She'd never lost that. Without her faith, she never would have survived the last two years. But hope—there just wasn't enough of that in her heart anymore.

Though she'd regret it in the morning, she let her thoughts travel, through picnics, birthday parties and quiet moments. To Rusty's contagious smile.

But then another smile stole into her thoughts, so surprising that she flipped over and sat up in bed. Brett Lancaster? The man was a stranger. A stranger who had no business being in her thoughts—or in this room where Rusty's memory still thrived.

Agitation had her wrapping her arms around her knees. She didn't want to remember the disaster their would-be date had been. But maybe God had chosen now to convict her heart over her deception in breaking the date.

Why hadn't she just gone out with Brett and gotten the whole annoying business over with? As adroit as she'd become at avoiding second dates, she already would have said goodbye to Mr. Lancaster and would be free until her next friend insisted on setting her up. Instead, guilt had forced her to reschedule.

Shaking her head, Tricia couldn't help smiling at the thought of Brett's mini bowling clinic. At the way his eyes crinkled in the corners when he laughed with-

Lani. But it was the memory of those same chocolate eyes focusing on her and widening with some indefinable emotion that made her as uncomfortable as it had at the bowling alley.

Suddenly, this rescheduled date felt like a huge mistake. What if Brett had the wrong idea about her, that she actually was open to a relationship? That couldn't have been further from the truth. He needed to understand that her heart was still committed to her husband.

Who are you trying to convince? She shook away the question and her uncomfortable guilt as she rushed over to the his-and-hers closets and opened one of the doors. On the side that was still *his,* the closet rod was empty except for a royal-blue jacket bearing the words "R and J Construction" and a sport coat. A lonely Detroit Lions football cap rested on the shelf.

Tricia grabbed the sport coat, Rusty's only dress jacket aside from the gray suit she'd buried him in, and pressed her face to the collar, inhaling his scent. Her nose burned. The room blurred. Drawing in the smell so deeply that her lungs ached, she held her breath until the survival instinct insisted she gasp. If only she could hold him there, deep inside of her. Her breath hitched as she realized his scent had already begun to fade. How long would it be until she couldn't smell him anymore, and she had nothing left of him?

So exhausted. For the first time in months, the effort of coping crushed her with its weight. The brave smile and strong words—parts of a facade that said she and the children were fine—crumbled around her. She wasn't fine. Rusty, Jr. certainly wasn't fine. His surliness grew more apparent every day, and he was beginning to act out. Lani seemed to curl deeper into herself each week and into her *Little House* books, where Ma and Pa always came home to Mary, Laura and Carrie. Only Max seemed oblivious, for he would never remember what he'd lost.

As the first tears in weeks came hot and furious, Tricia laid the sport coat aside, clasping the blue jacket and wrapping it around herself. She dropped back on the bed and drew her knees up to her chest, pulling the jacket tight beneath her chin. Again, she breathed Rusty's scent and fell into a troubled sleep, claiming the only warmth the love of her life could still bring her.

The organist at Hickory Ridge Community Church was still playing the postlude Sunday morning when Charity McKinley hurried up the side aisle, trying to catch Tricia before she could get out the door. Even sitting right near the back hadn't helped Tricia escape this time. She wondered if anyone would notice if she made a fast break for her station wagon.

"So tell me," Charity said as soon as she'd given her friend a quick hug.

Tricia glanced down quickly at the children, worried that Rusty, Jr. might repeat some of the last evening's antics if they mentioned Brett Lancaster.

"Mom, can we go talk to Reverend Bob and Mr.

Westin?'' Lani indicated with her head toward the minister and youth minister shaking hands with members in the vestibule.

Tricia didn't have any illusions her daughter wanted to have a heart-to-heart with grown-ups, but she nodded anyway. As expected, her children ran out to join Reverend Bob's granddaughter and Andrew Westin's children, who were giggling and banging hangers in the coatrack together. Discordant clanging and chatting voices filled the void as the organist stopped playing.

''How'd it go?'' Charity pressed again. ''What did you think of Brett? We're expecting a full report.''

Charity's husband, Rick, stepped up and caught the tail end of her comment. ''No, *we're* not. Only one of us is being too nosy for her own good.'' He dropped a kiss on Tricia's cheek. ''I hope you had a good time, but don't let her bully you into telling us about it.''

''Well, I never,'' Charity said with an impatient toe tap and a petulant expression that crumbled into a chuckle.

Her husband shook his head and rolled his eyes but gathered his spirited wife into his arms and kissed the top of her golden head. Tricia was still amazed by the transformation Charity had undergone when, first, she'd met Rick and, more importantly, she'd met the Lord close up. Even now the couple were still acting like newlyweds after more than two years. Charity gazed up lovingly at her husband before turning back to Tricia.

"Don't listen to him. He hates it when I set people up. He thinks I'm bad at it."

"Especially when you set up a friend with some guy somebody tried to set *you* up with a few years back."

"Jealous?" Charity gave him a sidelong glance. "Ignore him. I never went out with Brett. It's just that Jenny is dying for her brother to meet someone nice."

At the look of constrained curiosity, Tricia took pity on her matchmaker. "Sorry, there's not much to say. I met him, but we didn't go out yet. We had to reschedule."

Brett probably wouldn't have told the same story, but Tricia had given the gist of it. And no matter how uncomfortable it would be to go out after their embarrassing meeting, she'd resigned herself to going through with it. She owed him that much.

"Oh, that's too bad. When are you going? Have you decided what the two of you are going to do? Do you need us to watch the kids?"

Peppered by Charity's questions, Tricia felt a direct hit from the last one, which probably would have required her to tell the rest of the story about the date that didn't happen. "No," she answered too quickly. "I mean...I already asked Hannah."

Charity's eyes widened, and she opened her mouth to say something else, but Rick put his arm around her again. "Remember, sweetheart, matchmaking doesn't give you rights to all the details." He pressed his wife against his shoulder and turned to Tricia, his expression serious. "You're probably not into this stuff, anyway."

Once again, Rick had come to her rescue, the same way he'd been doing since Rusty died—both emotionally and financially. As much as she hated continuing to rely on him when she should have stood firmly on her own two size seven-and-a-half narrows, she appreciated the support. Losing Rusty had devastated them both. And Rick was probably no more prepared to watch her date other men than she was to begin a social life. His loyalty to his best friend's memory was still too strong.

"It's okay," she said when Rick seemed to expect Tricia to agree with his assumption about her reluctance to begin dating. "We haven't made firm plans yet."

Charity nodded. Tricia waved as the couple moved past her toward the exit. Finally, she let go of the breath she'd been holding. Didn't anyone understand that she *was* happy? Maybe not ecstatic, but she was content. How many people could say that? She had a nice home, a good church family, three beautiful children and a good start on a self-supportive future. It was enough for her. She just wished it was enough for all of her friends.

Brett took a deep, calming breath as he shuffled up the walk to the tiny white house, more nervous than he'd ever been for a date. A dozen times in the last six days, he'd considered canceling, worried that he was way out of his league dating a widowed mom. He'd even phoned Tuesday to call it off, but at the first sound of her voice, and the corresponding shiver in his spine, he'd heard himself firming up plans for their Friday date instead. Later, he'd scrambled to make sure his dad hadn't offered the tickets to someone else.

As he reached the front door, it flew open and a barefoot Max zipped out onto the porch. Then the boy stopped himself and extended his hand, as if he'd been carefully coached. "Hi, Mr. Brett."

"How ya doing, Max?" Brett gripped his hand. "Isn't the cement cold?"

"It's April now. That's almost summer. When it's sunny, we'll go swimming."

He returned the boy's grin but doubted his logic. Around chilly southeast Michigan, he didn't see any point in putting on a swimsuit until at least mid-June. Even now, his lined jacket felt no warmer than a windbreaker. He hauled the boy into his arms and opened the storm door.

A trim blonde with a long ponytail hurried across the living room and jerked to a stop in front of Brett. "Maxwell Thomas Williams, I told you not to go out that door in bare feet. What will your mother say?"

The smile on the young woman's lips took some of the steam from her firm tone. "You be good, or we won't watch movies and eat popcorn when your mom leaves."

Too busy to listen, Max tore to the kitchen table,

where his brother and sister were playing a board game. A chorus of moans filtered back to the living room.

The young woman glanced over her shoulder before turning back and extending her hand. "You must be Brett. Hi, I'm Hannah Woods, the baby-sitter."

"Good to meet you." As Brett shook her tiny hand, he wondered if she would be strong enough to handle the three Williams kids. But then he remembered that their mother was far smaller than this woman.

"Tricia will be out in a minute."

"Great."

He scanned the living room where a sofa, a television and an easy chair shared space with a smattering of framed family photos and snapshots on side tables and walls. All but the most recent shots featured a rusty-haired man with a friendly smile. Brett tried to keep a cool, mental distance from the pictures, only observing that he'd found the origin of the boys' hair color. But he couldn't shake the sensation of being watched.

"That was my daddy. He died," Lani said, pointing out the obvious, as she showed up beside him wearing fuzzy pink pajamas and smelling of baby shampoo.

"They're nice pictures." He hoped it was enough because he could find nothing better to say.

It must have been because the child then skipped around the partial wall that separated the living room from the eat-in kitchen, and rolled the die for her turn, adding a leg to her bug's body in the game. Next to her, Rusty, Jr. pointedly refused to glance at the guest in the living room.

Out of the corner of his eye, Brett saw movement from the hall, and when he would have expected a petite brunette, he saw only an even tinier Cindy Lou Who look-alike with blond ponytails and huge, dramatic green eyes.

Something in his gut clenched. Four? He was having a hard enough time reconciling the idea of going out with a woman who had three kids. But four?

"She's mine," Hannah said quickly. "That's Rebecca." The child looked up at her name being spoken but scrambled off to play under the kitchen table.

"Oh."

He wondered how he could have missed the resemblance now that she'd clarified it. Relief must have registered in his expression because Hannah smiled. He would have taken time to study the young woman, who couldn't have been old enough to be that child's mother, if not for the second person who appeared in the hallway.

Tricia wasn't dressed particularly fancy, just a pair of fitted jeans and a prim, turquoise sweater set. It pleased him that she had taken extra effort with her makeup—which she didn't need—and had clipped her hair back at her nape. Her hairstyle revealed a long expanse of perfect, fair skin on her neck.

Brett's mouth went dry. Until she shifted uncomfortably under his scrutiny, he wasn't even aware he'd been staring. What was he doing, acting like an infatuated teenager? He was neither, so he'd better get a grip before people started making mistaken assumptions.

She cleared her throat and glanced at the children playing in the kitchen before turning back to him. "Am I dressed okay? I've never been to a hockey game."

Okay enough to turn every male head at Joe Louis Arena, he figured. But he only said, "Sure, that's fine, unless you have a Steve Yzerman or Gordie Howe jersey."

He glanced down at his jeans and navy cardigan over a white turtleneck, trying not to grin at how long it had taken him to pick his outfit. "I left my jersey at home."

"You two had better get going," Hannah said as she rushed them toward the door. "Traffic's going to be terrible on the Lodge." The young woman didn't look at either of them, but a small smile appeared on her lips when she handed Tricia her coat.

Because Hannah was probably right about traffic on the John C. Lodge freeway, he hurried Tricia toward his SUV. He was relieved when she didn't comment on his luxury transportation, a concession to his former life.

He closed her door and crossed to the driver's seat. "Do you feel like we've just been dismissed?"

Tricia shot a glance at the closed curtains of the picture window and then turned to stare out the windshield. "Hannah just didn't want us to be late." As they pulled away from the curb, she sneaked another peek back, using the side-view mirror. "She's a great sitter. The kids will be fine. They'll have a great time, especially since she and Rebecca are spending the night."

Was she trying to convince him or her? He was tempted to reach over and squeeze her hand to reassure her, but he hesitated, worried she'd climb out of her skin if he touched her. Instead, he concentrated on merging onto Interstate 96 and tried changing the subject.

"I was surprised the little girl was hers. Hannah doesn't look old enough to be a mom."

"She isn't—or wasn't—really old enough, but she's a wonderful mom." Tricia settled back into the seat, finally relaxing. "Hannah was just seventeen when she got pregnant, but she's worked so hard to make the best of her difficult situation."

"I take it the dad isn't in the picture?"

Tricia shook her head but turned to face him. "She refused to name the father, even under pressure from some church members. I think it was especially hard on her, being the P.K."

"P.K.?"

"Preacher's Kid. She's the daughter of our minister, Reverend Bob Woods."

"I'd bet that was a huge church scandal." He hated it when Christians were the first to judge others. The poor girl had probably first been betrayed by a boy and then by the people in her church, the people she trusted. He knew what it was like to have the foundations of one's life—and even faith—ripped away. It tended to jade a person. He was proof of that.

"It was scandalous at first, but the church has been so supportive of Hannah, even of her decision to keep the baby instead of giving her up for adoption." Tricia was smiling when he glanced her way. "And you couldn't find a more devoted grandfather than Reverend Bob."

"Sounds like Hannah was pretty fortunate."

"She does her part, too, working hard to get her college degree and still being a great mom to Rebecca. She's pretty amazing."

"Yes, she is."

But he was no longer talking about the other young woman's situation, and he wondered if Tricia realized it. His date might have been amazed by Hannah's determination, but he was equally impressed with Tricia's. How had the woman beside him faced everything that had been thrown at her? Without trying to sound too interested, he'd plied Jenny for details about Tricia this week. How she'd survived her horrible loss two years before astounded him. His own injuries seemed trivial when compared to hers.

As if she, too, wondered where his thoughts had traveled, Tricia changed the subject again. "So you're Brett Lancaster. Are you any relation to the old movie star Burt Lancaster?"

Brett looked at the dash clock. "That's seventeen

minutes. I wondered how long it would take you to ask.''

"Was my time good or bad?''

"Pretty good. For the record, I'm not related to Burt Lancaster, and I've never seen *From Here to Eternity* beginning to end.''

Tricia's laugh was so sweet and musical that he wanted to come up with a comic monologue to make her do it again.

"I'm glad you made that clear.'' She paused. "Hmm, next subject. How'd you manage to get these tickets, anyway? I'd always heard it was impossible to get Detroit Red Wings tickets.''

"Ever heard of Lancaster Cadillac-Pontiac-GMC in Bloomfield Hills? I *am* related to that Lancaster. He's my dad.''

"I think I've heard of it.''

Her answer sounded noncommittal, as if she were neither impressed nor put off by the fact that his family had money. Well, she couldn't be that driven by money if she'd agreed to go out with a police officer.

"Dad has season tickets through his work that he mostly uses to take out clients.''

She turned to face him. "Do you go to games often?''

"Rarely. And don't get too excited about these tickets. This is one of the last regular-season games and attendance is sometimes low. If this were the end of next week during the first round of the Stanley Cup playoffs, we'd be out of luck in getting tickets.''

When he glanced at her again in his peripheral vision, she nodded. "I get it. I'm not supposed to be impressed, but can't I be, just a little? This is my first hockey game, ever, and it happens to be the Detroit Red Wings."

"Okay, just a little." He peeked at the tickets he'd stuck in the visor, glad he'd gone against his recent habit of declining his father's gifts for the strings that went with them. As he pulled behind the long line of cars taking the exit for Joe Louis Arena, he resigned himself to dealing with those strings later.

"Okay, be impressed now. Here's the Joe. Welcome to 'Hockeytown.'"

Chapter Three

Applause, cheers of "Hey, hey, Hockeytown" and the bass beat of some sixties rock anthem pounded in her ears as Tricia watched two players battle against the boards for the puck. Though air whooshed from a forward's lungs as he hit the glass barrier, he pushed away and skated behind the goal to recapture the loose puck.

The Detroit team was playing one of those new expansion teams with a name about as forgettable, at least according to Tricia's date, who doubled as her hockey interpreter. From their fifth-row seats, she could see, hear and feel every exciting bit of it.

"Let's go Red Wings," the crowd chanted, with Tricia and Brett joining in the chorus.

The exhilarating game—that had to be the reason for the way her pulse tripped and all of her nerve endings tingled, as if she'd suddenly awakened from an overlong nap. Taking another big bite of her Coney dog and wiping her mouth on her napkin, she shivered from the arena's refrigeration and wished she'd worn a heavier sweater.

"Cold?" As he asked, Brett draped her coat over her shoulders.

"Better. Thanks." Her shoulders warmed all over, but especially where his hands had brushed. She shook the sensation away, inhaling another breath of that strange, stale scent Brett had explained was the ice itself.

The buzzer sounded to mark the end of the second period. Fans scooted past them on their way up to the concession stands, but Brett and Tricia remained seated.

"Are you having a good time?" He turned in the cramped seats until his knees brushed hers. Amber specks like dots of confetti danced in his light brown eyes—the spots only noticeable from this close up.

"I am." She didn't want to lie. Tonight was the most fun she'd had on a date since…well, since she'd started dating again. It was so much better than those dreadful dinner dates she'd subjected herself to in the last year, with stilted conversations and self-conscious dining. Miserable in every way.

Strange, she could barely remember what it was like when she and Rusty had dated. It had been so long ago, and they'd both been so young and broke. This situation was different, so she should just enjoy it instead of making useless comparisons. Why compare what she couldn't have?

Tonight wasn't a serious date, anyway. Maybe that's why she was enjoying herself. While some of the men she'd been out with had been so nervous and intense that she'd worried they would propose before the waiter brought the main course, Brett seemed relaxed. In his element, even.

He didn't appear to expect more from her than to enjoy the game and, maybe, to learn the definitions of "face-off," "blue line" and "icing." The last term he insisted wasn't what went on a fudge cake, either. He'd told her there would be a quiz later, which she fully intended to ace.

"Well, what's the verdict?" he asked as the Zamboni made its first wet pass around the ice. "Does hockey pass the muster?"

"Absolutely." So did the company, though she didn't mention that. "I'll never be able to flip past a hockey game on TV again without stopping and comparing it to this. Hockey's different in person."

"It's also a different experience in the nosebleed seats, but I'd just as soon skip that joy, if you don't mind. Especially the racing pulse and lack of breath."

She raised an eyebrow at him. "Afraid of heights?"

"Not afraid, exactly. I just prefer to keep my feet on God's green earth is all."

A chuckle bubbled low in her belly, and Tricia couldn't stop it from frothing over. She felt guilty enjoying herself this much—almost too much. Were widows allowed to smile this often? Brett made a nasty face at her but finally laughed.

He shrugged. "Really, I like to watch the game better from up close, even if it's harder to see the strategies, the cool passes and great screens."

She shook her head at his funny bravado. Typical guy, he wouldn't admit to being anything but fearless. "The game's probably harder to see when you're breathing into a brown paper bag or hanging your head between your knees."

"There's that, too," Brett agreed. But something farther across the lower bowl of fan seats must have caught his attention because he looked away.

A videotape started playing on the four-sided scoreboard high above center ice, with Red Wings players scoring goals against various teams. Cheers and whoops erupted each time the tape showed the players in red and white firing the puck past an opposing goalie.

The next squeal Tricia heard came from her own lips, surprising her. Attending this game had been so much easier than she'd expected when Brett had first suggested it. At least this professional sport was hockey, rather than football and Rusty's beloved Detroit Lions. Rusty had always said he would take the children to a Lions' game when they were a little older. Just something else in a long list of things that would never happen now.

The temptation to grow maudlin filled her until she glanced at Brett. Turning back from whatever he'd been studying before, he patted her hand on the arm-rest and then lifted his soda from the seat's drink holder. "I don't know about you, but I'm having a great time."

"Me, too," she answered, trying not to react to what had been only a friendly touch. A buddy touch, nothing for her neck to get all warm about. She ought to feel lucky he hadn't slapped her on the back the way men were wont to do with their friends to act chummy.

"And I think we should go out again."

She wished he'd slapped her on the back instead of saying that. It had knocked the wind out of her, anyway. Her cheeks grew as heated as her neck, so Tricia took the coward's way out and turned to sip her own cola.

"We'll have to do something besides watch hockey, though. We'd never get playoff tickets." He paused as if waiting for her to answer before he spoke again. "But if you don't think that's a good idea…"

As he allowed his words to trail away, letting her off the hook, her mind raced. Did she want an escape? This dating thing had no future, but they were having fun together, and she couldn't remember the last time she'd enjoyed herself so much in adult company. And she really did need to get out more. They could probably even grow to be great pals, like some of the men attending this game together, if she only gave them a chance.

She was still convincing herself when Brett shook his head. "I'm sorry. I don't mean to pressure—"

"I'd like that."

Brett stared at her a few seconds and then grinned. "Well, good. That'll be great." He touched her hand again, and she had the strange feeling the brief caress wasn't one a couple of hockey buddies might share. Their gazes met, and an awareness unfolded inside of her, until she forced herself to look away.

Obviously, she hadn't explained the parameters of their new friendship to him, and he'd probably misunderstood her interest. With a quick brush to expel the tickle on her hand, she turned to him to clear up the misunderstanding.

However, whatever had caught her date's attention near the Red Wings' team box earlier had grabbed it again. The way his body tensed, he appeared at a strange full-alert. Tricia saw them then, several men, swilling tall plastic cups of beer and wearing jerseys for teams that weren't playing. They crowded close around the tunnel through which hockey players were emerging from their locker rooms.

Someone must have alerted security guards to a possible disturbance because they were making their way across the stands. Before the guards reached the tunnel, though, one of the men upended his cup, narrowly missing a player.

At once, fists started flying—not from the players, who were being ushered by their teammates toward the ice, but from fans who took exception to the treatment of their hometown heroes. A huddle of bodies appeared from nowhere as reinforcements leaped into the fray and other fans stood to catch the action.

Brett came out of his seat just as quickly, but his movements were automatic—fast glances toward the exits and a hand reaching reflexively for his right hip. Coming away with nothing. A gun? A shiver clambered up Tricia's spine, and bile backed up in her throat. Had he been reaching for a holster? Only after he patted his sweater-covered hip a few times did Brett lower into his seat again.

Further down the stands, security guards removed the instigators from the arena, but Tricia barely noticed. Brett shoved both hands back through his hair and shook his head as he turned back to her.

"Now that was embarrassing," he said.

He seemed to want her to say something, but she could only stare, her blood now as cold in her veins as her cheeks from the arena's refrigerated chill. Her pulse raced, and an icy sweat covered her hands. When she started to speak, she choked.

Brett's eyes widened, and he reached over to pat her back, but she jerked away from his touch. The situation that had felt so comfortable before became awkward, and his nearness, suffocating.

Finally, she found her voice. "I need you to tell me something. Are you a cop?"

"I can't believe no one ever told you I was a trooper," Brett said with an exasperated sigh as he pulled out of the parking structure nearly an hour later. What he wanted to say was *I can't believe it matters so much that I'm a cop,* but from her stiff posture and wringing hands, he'd be a fool not to see that it did.

She sat still in the car seat next to him, the same way she'd been for most of the game's third period and even during the walk through the tunnel that connected the arena to the parking garage. Jubilant fans had packed in all around them, still cheering and making the cattle sounds of the exit ritual, but Tricia had been eerily silent. Her strange reaction cut him a lot deeper than it should have, like history coming back to bite him on the backside. But he wouldn't sit back and wait for it to happen this time.

"No one mentioned my job at all?" he asked, still incredulous. "Nothing about me moving to Livingston County so I could be close to work at the Brighton Post?"

She released a long, slow breath. "Charity didn't tell me anything about what you did."

What Tricia didn't say, what she couldn't possibly have known, made more difference to him than what she'd said. Had Jenny mentioned that he worked for the Michigan State Police, her friend would have passed that along to Tricia when they'd arranged the date.

Of anyone, his sister, who'd followed her own heart into nursing, should have understood his need to follow his, especially after Claire called off the wedding. But this was proof that even his sister was ashamed of the career that had become so much a part of his identity. Why should she be any different from the rest of the family?

"What exactly did your friend tell you about me?" He had to unclench his jaw to continue. "No, let me guess. Decent guy, twenty-nine, not a jerk, without any facial disfigurement. Goes to church. Has a job so he won't expect you to pay for the movie tickets. That's all, right?"

A strange sound, like an ironic chuckle, erupted in her throat. "That's about it."

"I can't believe that. Jenny told me you worked part-time at Kroger, you were taking college classes, and you wanted someday to own a gourmet cooking store in Milford." About him, his sister had purposely mentioned nothing. "If she didn't tell you what I did, then why didn't you ask?"

Tricia shrugged, her silence answering for her. It didn't matter to her how he earned his living when she never intended to see him more than once. One blind date. No second one. Obviously, something had gone awry in her plan if she'd agreed to go out with him again. He remembered her reluctance to answer when he'd asked. Now it didn't matter, anyway. She'd changed her mind about him. All because he was a cop.

His fingers tightened on the steering wheel. "I don't get it. Why did you agree to be set up when it's obvious you didn't want to go?"

She sighed again. "It was easier than saying no and

having Charity try to convince me. And it was easier to let someone do something for me than to let them feel sorry for me."

Something struck inside him that he might have called a connection if he weren't so determined to stay angry with the whole situation. "That's why I agreed, too, but I made Jenny wheedle first."

"And then I stood you up."

The sides of his mouth pulled up against his will. "Yep, that's the way I remember it." He paused, searching for a safe topic. Since she'd finally started talking, he didn't want to risk making her clam up again. "Hey, I think it's time for that hockey quiz."

Out of the corner of his eye, he saw her turn slightly toward him, so he took it as a go-ahead. "What is the definition of a forecheck?"

"Hey, that one wasn't on the study guide. I protest."

"Okay, okay. A player forechecks when he blocks the progress of an opponent in his own defensive zone. So, what's a face-off?"

"I know that one. That's when two players from opposite teams stand in one of those circles and fight to get control of the puck." She settled back into her seat, satisfied with herself.

Brett tried to continue the hockey quiz, but another question ate at him until he finally couldn't resist asking it. "Tell me, how many blind dates have you been on…lately?" When she tightened, he was glad he hadn't said "since your husband died."

At first she didn't answer, but finally she gave an exaggerated shrug. "I don't know. Maybe fourteen."

"Fourteen? Really?"

"It's strange. I've been out with more people in the last year than I had in my whole life…before."

He wasn't the only one dancing around the subject of her late husband. "In the last year? That's more than one a month. I wouldn't have thought there'd be that many single guys around."

She chuckled at that. "Not just single guys, single Christian guys. Remember?" For a second, she appeared relaxed, with her shoulders curving forward. "Almost every one of my friends knew someone I just had to meet. Some don't realize that just because a guy has a strong faith doesn't mean he'll be the best date—for me, anyway."

"Kissed a lot of frogs, have you?"

She shook her head. "That's not what I meant."

At her reaction, melancholy settled over Brett, though he'd only intended to lighten the mood with his joke. She probably hadn't been kissed at all since becoming a widow, and he didn't like the thought of this beautiful woman having no haven in someone's arms. A voice inside suggested his arms might be a perfect fit, but he tried to ignore that nonsense. He was no more ready to leap into a relationship again than she appeared to be.

They drove in silence a few minutes as Interstate 696 merged into I-96, and they neared the Milford

Road exit. Finally, Brett asked the question that had been twirling through his mind.

"I know you've had fourteen first dates recently, but how many second dates have you had?" Her sudden intake of breath showed she'd realized what he was really asking. Would she or wouldn't she still go out again with him?

"I'm so sorry. If only I'd known—"

"What do you have to be sorry about?" He interrupted her to delay the kiss-off that was building. "You didn't answer the question. How many?"

Her word came out like a whisper. "None."

"But you said you would—"

This time she interrupted him, as if to prevent him from reminding her what she'd said. "I won't be able to go out with you again."

Frustration melded with resentment over past and present slights until Brett couldn't take it anymore. "What's the big deal about me being a cop? You'd think I was a convicted felon or something."

"Your job involves risk."

He acknowledged her comment with a shrug. That was a given. A trooper took a certain amount of risk every time he climbed into his patrol car, every time he stepped out of it to ticket a driver for a traffic violation. He accepted it as part of the job but didn't waste energy worrying about it.

"And your point is?"

She scooted closer to the passenger door. "Did anyone tell you about how Rusty died?"

His head jerked and his stomach tightened at her question. They'd both been tiptoeing around the subject all night, and she'd just waded in waist deep. Now that she'd named him, the dead man seemed to be here, squeezed in the SUV between their two bucket seats. "A construction accident, right?"

"Yeah. He was walking the walls on the project, something that's dangerous even in the best conditions. But that morning it was damp from the last night's storm. It was windy. Rusty still thought he needed to be up there walking atop a two-story wall that was only three-and-a-half inches wide. He lost his balance. He hit a pile of bricks at the bottom."

By the time she reached the end of the story, he wished he hadn't encouraged her to tell it. She stared blankly into the darkness, reliving a moment no wife should have to endure. His hands ached so much to gather her into his arms that he gripped the wheel so he wouldn't succumb to the need and drive them right off the road.

The worst part was her husband's accident sounded preventable. The man had no business being where he was—Tricia had nearly said so herself. What kind of idiot would have taken that chance when he had a family to think about? When he had someone like Tricia to come home to?

"I'm sorry" was the only decent thing he could think to say, the only response that didn't include referring to her beloved husband as an irresponsible imbecile.

Tricia nodded at the windshield but didn't look at him. "Rusty was always taking risks."

She said no more. She didn't have to. In her round-about way, Tricia had finally told him what he needed to know. His career mattered—a lot—because of the risks he accepted as part of the job. She'd buried her husband because of the risks he took. Now she didn't want any part of someone else who took them.

Brett tried to focus on the road as traffic slowed to twenty-five miles per hour at the Milford village limit, but he couldn't keep from glancing at her stoic profile. Still, he felt compelled to defend his career choice that was as much a part of him as those children were part of her.

"I don't ever remember wanting to be anything else," he began, waiting for her to turn to him, but she didn't. "Whenever Jenny and I played cops and robbers with our brother, Kyle, I was always the cop. Jenny always had to be the nurse." The notion struck him as strange that Kyle had always played the robber, fitting for the failure he'd turned out to be.

"I even chose criminal justice as one of my majors in college. Business was the other." He paused, remembering and regretting decisions he'd made. "But then Dad needed a new business manager at the dealership, and Claire and I decided it would be a better choice, so I—"

"Claire?"

He should have been glad that she was finally involved in the conversation, but he hated that she'd picked up on that little detail, and the fact that he'd even mentioned her. "My ex-fiancée."

"Oh."

Good. At least she hadn't asked for gory details. He couldn't remember a time when he didn't love Claire Davis, and he wanted to do nothing but forget her now.

"Anyway, after that was over, I took the Civil Service written test. I tested twice before I was invited to take the physical agility test and then the oral board interview."

"Sounds like an intense selection process."

Shocked that she seemed interested at all, he continued. "That's not the half of it. I still had to go through a psych evaluation, a drug test and a complete physical before I could go to the Michigan State Police Recruit School."

"Was it all worth it?"

He smiled in the darkness before he answered her. "Oh, yeah. I get up every day, looking forward to going to work. I love all of it, patrolling the highway, working with the other troopers, even seeing so many sides of people. You just become so engrossed in it. It defines who you are."

"It sounds like the job suits you."

"It does."

Brett's chest loosened as he pulled to a stop across the street from her house. Maybe she would relax, too, and give him a chance. At least he hadn't been stupid and talked about putting his life in his fellow troopers' hands and holding theirs in his. Not everyone could handle that reality, and Tricia probably was one of those.

"I had a nice time tonight," Tricia started.

Brett heard the "but" before she had a chance to say it. "Wait, Tricia." Suddenly he needed to prove himself to her in the same way he'd being trying to show his family he could make more of a difference in police work than he ever could with the Lancaster money.

"You know, we're only going out as friends. It's not as if either of us has anything long-term in mind, right?" He saw that she was about to interrupt, so he pressed on. "And we have fun together. You said that yourself. Why don't we just play it by ear? You know, casual. I don't know about you, but I really needed a night out."

Tricia tilted her head, as if she was considering his offer. He hated that it mattered so much that she say yes.

Finally, she shook her head. "It wouldn't be a very good idea."

"Come on, Tricia. You know you want to. And I like you. I think you like me, too."

But she only shook her head again.

His chest felt heavy as a disappointment too intense for a simple rejection following just one date festered inside him. "Then tell me why."

She expelled what sounded like a long-held breath. "Going out with you would be a constant reminder of all I've lost."

Chapter Four

Tricia turned the knob as quietly as she could, but the front door still squeaked, causing four small figures on the living room floor to jerk before they snuggled deeper in their character sleeping bags. Following the only remaining light into the kitchen, she found Hannah hunched at the table over a thick textbook, a cup of tea set within arm's reach.

"Did you have a nice time?" Hannah's voice was barely above a whisper.

Tricia nodded and then shrugged. "It was probably a bad idea to go."

"You liked him, didn't you?"

A startled breath escaped her before she could cover it. How could someone so young be so intuitive? But then she answered her own question: pain could make a person grow up fast. "No, it isn't that," she answered after a pause too long for Hannah not to have drawn her own conclusions.

Hannah nodded and moved over to the sink, pulling a second mug from the cupboard and pouring hot water into it. She waited until she'd dunked a bag of chamomile in to steep and had set it in front of Tricia before she spoke again. "Then what is it?"

"He's a trooper for the Michigan State Police." But it wasn't that image of a man in uniform that sneaked into her thoughts then. This was the Brett she'd known only as a distracted bowler and a hockey expert. His smile was inviting and his laughter contagious.

"Oh."

Hannah's single-syllable answer pulled Tricia back from her forbidden thoughts. So strange that the young woman instinctively seemed to know why Brett's job would matter so much to her.

"I'm surprised you didn't know that before you agreed to go out with him," Hannah said.

Absently, Tricia swished the tea bag in her mug, squeezed it out and set it on the table top. "There was some confusion about matchmakers not passing along the information. If I had known, I wouldn't have gone."

"I know. But you did."

Neither spoke for several minutes. Tricia sipped the bland tea, wishing her thoughts could be equally benign. But the truth was, Hannah's first observation was dead on—Tricia liked him—and now she was having trouble reconciling this man she liked with the one she imagined wearing a badge. And trudging up to car windows, never knowing what kind of armed thug might be inside.

"Did you enjoy your first hockey game?" Hannah asked, glancing at the wall clock instead of Tricia. "I caught the score on the news. Looked like a good game."

"It was. Everything was so fast—the skating, the passes and the goals. I couldn't believe how exhilarating it was." Tricia was equally surprised at how animated she became, just describing a sport she'd known nothing about until tonight. So she backtracked. "There was just so much action."

Hannah met her gaze then. "It's okay if you had fun, you know. Even if you kind of liked Brett. Rusty wouldn't mind. He'd want you to be happy."

But Tricia shook her head, her eyes burning with tears she refused to cry. "It wasn't like that."

"Then what was it like?"

"You know how many horrible blind dates I've been out on? Well, this time I was having fun, mostly because it was so laid-back. No pressure." She paused. "But that was before I found out what he did."

"Well…before…maybe you were finally feeling that you're ready to start really dating again."

Tricia took another sip of her lukewarm tea and pondered that possibility. "No, I don't think so. I don't think I'll ever be ready. Besides, if I were, I wouldn't feel so guilty about it."

"Like you're betraying Rusty?" She didn't wait for Tricia's nod before she added, "Dad says he always feels like that when he takes a woman out."

"Reverend Bob is dating again?" As incredulous as she was that the widower was finally having a social life, Tricia was relieved to talk about something besides her own nightmares of being set up. Then, remembering her son's reaction to Brett, she studied the minister's only daughter. "How do you feel about that?"

It was Hannah's turn to be reticent. "Oh, I suppose it's time," she said with a negligent wave. "Mom's been gone more than five years now. Dad's only been out with a few women—all of them from other churches, for obvious reasons."

"I can see why he'd want to do that." Dating, though a tricky subject for all divorced or widowed church members, was extra sensitive for a minister. If she needed an example, she had only to think of youth minister Andrew Westin and his wife, Serena, who'd had to weather accusations of sexual impropriety when they dated. She didn't envy Reverend Bob the microscope he would be under as each potential relationship warmed or cooled. "Have you liked any of the women he's dated?"

Hannah made a noncommittal sound in her throat. "They've been nice, but none of them have been quite right for him." Her lips turned up in a sheepish grin. "At least in my opinion."

Tricia sensed that Hannah would never find a

woman good enough for her father. An emptiness filled Tricia as she realized that was exactly how Rusty, Jr. felt about her, how Lani and Max may have felt, too. Rusty, Jr. had been acting out more than the other two, but he was the only one who'd convinced himself he was now the man of the house. She only wished he could be her little boy.

"It's got to be so hard for your dad to move on." Restlessness making it impossible for her to sit any longer, Tricia stood and stepped around the half wall to watch her three sweet children and little Rebecca sleep. "For me, it's impossible."

While Tricia expected Hannah to respond to that comment, or even to finally reveal something of her own painful secrets, Hannah rounded the table and stood next to her.

"It takes a special kind of person to have a career in law enforcement."

Tricia glanced at her and Hannah smiled, having slyly returned to an earlier subject. The conversation had come full circle, right back to Brett.

"I'm sure it does, Hannah, but—"

"No, listen. These are everyday heroes. They put their uniforms on each day and go to work, knowing at any moment they might be called upon to be heroic."

Something unsettling moved inside her, but was it fear or a temptation to buy into what Hannah was saying? She couldn't dispute any of it. Still she couldn't go as far as to say that Brett's career didn't matter to her. Even if she was ready to have a relationship with anybody—and there were so many glaring signals she was not—then his badge would flare like a fiery red stop sign to discourage her. The career, which Brett freely admitted defined him, involved more risk than Rusty ever took, even on his best daredevil day. And she'd had enough risk to last a lifetime.

"Well, I'm glad people like that are out there, aren't you?" Tricia asked, hoping Hannah would drop the matter. Sure, she hoped police officers were out there somewhere, but not close to home, where she had to be the one to worry about them. Or him.

With a wave, Hannah headed off to sleep in Lani's frilly pink bedroom, leaving Tricia to her nighttime ritual of checking the locks on the front and back doors—twice—and flipping off the lights. But tonight she didn't want to be alone in the dark with her thoughts. She'd discovered a few things about herself that she wasn't ready to swallow.

For one thing, she was lonelier than she'd realized. Her other discovery was that she could enjoy herself in the company of a man other than Rusty. She refused to take it a step further and admit she could be susceptible to attraction, especially to someone like Brett.

She shook away the thoughts as she climbed into bed and squeezed her eyes shut. The disquiet inside her, though, refused to subside. She longed for an escape from this day when she'd so easily forsaken the husband she'd promised to love forever, when she'd agreed to the unthinkable—a second date—whether it would ever happen or not. But as she closed her eyes, she had no doubt her troubled thoughts would follow her into her dreams.

Just before the 6:00 a.m. beginning of Saturday's day shift, Brett slammed his locker door and set aside his shiny black duty belt that, like fellow troopers, he often fondly referred to as a "Sam Brown." But not today. He wasn't in the mood to refer to anything fondly today.

"What's with you, Lancaster?"

Brett jerked his head to the sound of Trooper Joey Rossetti's voice, knowing full well that only somebody with a death wish would call the former linebacker his lifelong neighborhood nickname instead of "Joe." He was just surly enough this time to test the theory. "Lay off, would you?"

"I could." Joe nodded a few times as if considering it, but then he shook his head. "But then if I couldn't watch you banging around in here, what would I do for entertainment?" One side of Joe's mouth pulled up in a smirk before it returned to its usual hard line. "Really, do you…um…need—anything I can do?"

Can you pound it into my family's heads that my days at the dealership are over? Can you make paper cuts the most dangerous part of my job so Tricia Williams will go out with me? But he only said, "Nah, it's nothing," as he buttoned the top button of his navy uniform shirt over his Kevlar vest, knotted his gray tie and pinned on his silver badge.

"Yeah, it sounds like nothing."

Brett put on his duty belt, making a production of

checking to see that all of its contents were in place—pepper spray, collapsible baton, handcuffs case, mini-flashlight, radio and extra magazines. Then he patted his hands over the .40-caliber semiautomatic pistol at his right hip. At least it was here this time.

Apparently, Trooper Rossetti was tired of his silence because he tried again. "This isn't still about Claire, is it? She didn't come crawling back, did she?"

The venomous look Brett tossed at his buddy, who he'd once tapped to serve as best man at his defunct wedding, must have spoken for him because Joe nodded. "Good. I keep telling you there are plenty of fish in the sea. No use reeling the same one in all the time."

That coming from a guy who'd often vowed he couldn't be dragged to the altar with anything less threatening than a howitzer.

"Sounds like something you should put on a greeting card."

"Ya think?" The younger trooper flashed a grin that he'd used for bait on his own frequent "fishing" trips. "So then I have a career in greeting cards after I lay down my badge?"

They both laughed at that, and Brett slapped Joe on the back as he passed. Neither of them would ever turn in his uniform without a fight. Not for anybody.

"You were at the Red Wings game last night, weren't you?" Joe asked as he finished putting on his uniform. "I saw something about a fight that broke out in the stands."

"Yeah, I was there, but—" he paused for a few

seconds "—I didn't have my gun." Brett wasn't accustomed to breaking rules, and this one was a law
that required State Police troopers to carry a firearm
at all times.

"Hey, don't sweat it. It happens sometimes. Besides, the last time I went to a concert in Detroit, security made me lock up my gun, anyway."

Brett pushed the door to head out into the squad
room, relieved he'd managed to get through the conversation without having to discuss his miserable date.
But Joe followed him out the door.

"How'd your date go?" he asked from behind.

When Brett jerked his head to the side, he caught
Joe studying him with a knowing smile. He'd figured
out the source of Brett's sour mood. Brett shouldn't
have expected to keep a secret for long, especially
from the trooper who used to be his partner on the
midnight shift. He was glad now to be on days, where
he didn't have to share his car or his thoughts with
anyone.

But since Joe wouldn't go away, he filled him in on
the story, even the part about him going for his non-
existent gun.

"So why are you wasting your time and energy on
a woman who refuses to date a cop?"

Brett's shrug must not have been a good enough
answer because Trooper Rossetti was still looking at
him as if he was daft when their patrol cars passed on
the way out of the parking lot. That sure appeared to
be the question of the day: why was he completing
this exercise in futility?

He pondered that as he examined the car ahead of him at the stoplight, the one with the expired license plates. With a few keystrokes on his laptop, he connected with the Law Enforcement Information Network's direct link to the Michigan Secretary of State's office to run a license plate check. Because the driver had an otherwise clean driving record, he gave him a break and didn't pull him over.

Brett wished it was that easy to dismiss his questions regarding Tricia Williams. They continued to bug him as he merged onto the interstate, watching the cars' brake lights flash as drivers reduced their speed the way they always did until they were a few miles past him. The last thing he needed was to risk another rejection, especially over a career choice he'd already suppressed for one woman.

Been there, done that, bought the postcard, burned it.

He'd already turned himself inside out trying to please Claire and his parents, trying to be the business manager he wasn't. Could he ever give up his work, his identity for someone else again? No. An emphatic no.

Wait, he needed to back up a bit. No one had *asked* him to do any identity switching lately, so why was he letting it bother him as if she'd demanded that he become a flower arranger or something to suit her? Besides, even if Tricia wasn't opposed to dating a police officer—a risk-taker—then he'd still have the elephant-size issue of having to compete with her late husband. Who could compete with a memory? And why would he want to?

"Central has a two-car PDA in Brighton Township," came the radio dispatch to all area police agencies.

"Central…one-four-four-seven…I'm southbound 96 at Pleasant Valley."

"One-four-four-seven, copy on the last."

Having been given the go-ahead by central dispatch to handle the property damage accident, Brett flipped on the car's red spinning overhead light that troopers often called a "gumball." He maneuvered through traffic to the accident scene near the Grand River Avenue exit. At least the work would occupy his thoughts. Adrenaline pumped in his veins, pushing his speed faster. Finally, he parked his car across the asphalt to block off the road. Leaving the overhead on, he climbed out of his car and put on his hat.

Though there were no injuries, this was one of the types of accidents Brett hated seeing. A dazed-looking grandfatherly gentleman stood at the side of the road, rubbing his bruised forehead. The man's crumpled car rested perpendicularly to the highway across two lanes, as if he'd tried to bisect it. Much more likely, he'd tried to change lanes and had cut off another driver—the one who was flailing his arms and creating his own dictionary of expletives while circling his damaged red convertible.

Brett approached the older man first and flipped open his metal portfolio with accident report forms inside. "Sir, I'm Trooper Lancaster from the Michigan State Police. Can you tell me what happened here?"

"I can tell you," said the other man, beefy and middle-aged, as he marched toward them.

But Brett raised his hand to stop him. "Sir, you're going to have to wait your turn."

"I don't want to wait." A huge vein thrummed at his temple, the blue stripe magnified because of his nearly bald head. "This idiot—"

"Sir—" Brett straightened, pushing his shoulders back and staring down the other man. "I said you'll have to wait. Please return to your car and let me complete this man's information. Then I'll take yours." He paused when the driver stood there looking at him incredulously, as if he'd just handcuffed him for the fun of it. He could do that, if the guy caused him trouble. "Unless you want to turn this small incident into a big one."

Apparently, the guy didn't want to because he harrumphed and did as the trooper had told him, giving Brett the chance to take a report from the older man.

"Union-Victor-David-six-two-four," he called the license plate letters and numbers into the radio attached at his shoulder. Then he read the man's name from his driver's license. "Walker...Gene."

Defeated didn't begin to describe the way the man looked, and Brett was only going to add to that when he cited him for an improper lane change. This accident would probably end Mr. Walker's driving years, would end his freedom, and Brett hated the role he played in that final drive. It seemed as if God took an awful lot away from people as they got on in years. Lucky for him, he'd experienced it early so it wouldn't come as a surprise.

The rest of his shift crept by after that. Just a few speeding tickets to write up, and he cited one driver for passing on the shoulder, his personal pet peeve. But none of it was enough to distract him from what was really on his mind. Though futile, he felt he had something to prove to Tricia Williams. He didn't like the way she lumped him together with every guy who'd ever faced danger in his job or life. He resented being thought of as reckless. In fact, those things bothered him more than that the lovely widow had traveled shotgun in his thoughts all day.

By the time he'd parked his car that night in the lot behind the post, he'd come to a decision. He might not have been able to convince his family that he was meant to be in community service rather than high-end retail, but maybe he could persuade one woman that she couldn't judge all men based on her late husband's actions.

He wanted to help her see the value in scratching below the surface when she met people, of looking beyond titles and initial reactions. His mission did sway from true altruism in that *he* happened to be the person he didn't want her to dismiss too quickly. But he'd never claimed to not have a self-serving side.

And Brett knew just the place to make his next "first impression."

Chapter Five

Late again, Tricia rushed the children into the rear church pew Sunday morning, her emotions still strained from the failure of their Saturday fishing adventure. Why had she even tried? And why had Rusty, Jr. insisted on her getting a fishing license and getting out his dad's special fishing rod if he only planned to criticize her casting, her hook baiting and everything else she tried?

He seemed to be punishing her for letting his father die, for trying to replace him—as if she ever could—and maybe even for enjoying herself on that date with Brett. As much as she wanted to mourn with her son the way she usually did for losses no child should have to face, she was tired this morning, and she was resentful. She wouldn't be going out with Brett again, so she wished Rusty, Jr. would just give her a break.

Tricia grabbed her hymnal and flipped to the right

page only to have Max tug it from her hands. She'd already begun flipping through the pages of another when she glanced at the opposite end of the back pew.

And she saw him.

Her hands felt frozen to the book, but her insides were just the opposite, still frigid but fluid. What was he doing here? To avoid staring, she focused on the lyrics and bars of musical notes.

"Mom, Mr. Brett is over there," Max whispered too loudly as usual.

This time Tricia jerked her head to look at the object of her son's loud announcement, hoping Brett hadn't heard it. Maybe he'd packed his ears with cotton that morning. *It could happen.* But even if by some amazing coincidence he'd managed to miss it, he couldn't have missed Max climbing up on the pew to point and wave.

Brett grinned sheepishly and waved back. Tricia's own smile was apologetic as she wrestled Max until his feet were back on the floor.

But Brett only winked and returned to his hymnal, his endearing off-key voice contributing to the song about being near to God. Did he feel the Lord's presence when he sang it? She didn't know about Brett, but the only presence she sensed right now was his. Why did he make her so uncomfortable? He couldn't have come to Hickory Ridge just to see her, anyway. She ignored the voice inside that wished he had.

Tricia was relieved when Reverend Bob asked the congregation to turn to the Book of Ruth.

''After their husbands died, Ruth and Orpah were widows and among the most vulnerable people in their day. Their mother-in-law, Naomi, told them to return to their own people, the Moabites, so they could find husbands to provide for them. Orpah did leave, but what did Ruth do instead?'' Reverend Bob paused the way he always did, for effect rather than an answer.

''She reached out to the mother of her dead husband,'' he finally supplied. ''Ruth said to her, 'For where you go I will go, and where you lodge I will lodge. Your people shall be my people, and your God, my God.'''

The familiar passage usually comforted her, but not today. The words and message bothered her as much as Brett's presence on the other end of the pew. Suddenly she was reliving the days and months following Rusty's death. Her parents had been a constant support to her then. She didn't know what she would have done without them.

But what if the situation would have been reversed? What if she had been the one to die instead of Rusty? Her husband had never had a family of his own to turn to in his grief. Would her parents have welcomed Rusty and become his people as Naomi had done for Ruth? With that answer, resentments from years past came hurtling back so quickly that Tricia braced herself to withstand the onslaught.

Her parents had never considered Rusty good enough for their only daughter and never missed an opportunity to let him know it. They'd blamed him for her decision to choose marriage over college. Didn't they understand she'd made a decision for love? She hadn't regretted it then, when she and Rusty had struggled for every dime they earned. And she didn't regret it now, even…after everything.

That same fierce need to protect her husband from her parents' criticisms filled her again. Too bad no one had been there to protect him from hers. How could she blame them when she hadn't been a supportive wife? *One of these days you're going to get yourself killed, and then I'll never forgive you.* She'd spoken those words in anger on a day when his injury had been minor—just a nail through his hand that time. The things she'd said had come back to haunt her the day she'd lost him forever. Some things a person could never take back.

Maybe she couldn't draw that hateful message back into her lungs, but she could protect her husband's memory and the love on which they'd built a marriage and a family. How could she have lost sight of that? How had she allowed herself to enjoy spending time with Brett—no matter how nice he was—when she was still so very much in love with Rusty? It betrayed his memory to forget so soon.

As Reverend Bob closed his sermon with soul-searching words leading to the invitation, Tricia glanced over at Brett again, ignoring the jolt at catching him watching her. She couldn't allow herself to react to another man.

Rusty deserved a widow who could truly grieve for

him, not just someone who could bide her time until a decent mourning period had passed. She planned to be the wife he deserved, and that meant not having thoughts beyond friendship for any man—Brett included. If she was so committed to her decision, why then did she feel so sad?

"Tricia, wait up," Brett called after her as she and the children crossed the parking lot toward her car.

Wishing they'd walked faster so she could have avoided meeting him, Tricia turned to let him catch up. She stilled herself as she waited. Unfortunately, she couldn't steady her breathing. A chorus of "Hi, Mr. Brett's"—with Rusty, Jr.'s noticeably missing—filled the air before Tricia even got a word out.

"Hi, Brett."

"Hi."

Tricia swallowed hard, determined not to fidget under the intensity of his gaze. Did he use that same brilliant smile when he stopped speeding female motorists? She hoped not, or they probably would be repeat offenders just to have him ticket them again.

Lani and Max saved them both from an awkward pause by stepping past their mother and crowding around Brett.

"Did you see my Sunday school class?" Max asked as Brett lifted him up. "It's the biggest one."

"They're all the same size in the Family Life Center," Lani added sardonically.

That only earned Lani a quick knuckle rub on the

noggin before he affectionately brushed the child's short, dark hair back from her face. Something warm spread inside Tricia's heart as she watched the man's kindness toward her children. But then she caught sight of Rusty, Jr., his posture rigid as he held back from the others. As if her nerves weren't already jittery enough.

"I didn't, uh, know you were planning to visit our church." Tricia took a step backward as she spoke— closer to Rusty, Jr. and farther from Brett.

His eyes widened, but Brett didn't try to close the distance. "I've been visiting a few places. I didn't get a chance to mention it the other night."

He politely didn't expound on the reason he didn't get to talk about it, but they both knew. They'd been too busy discussing her husband's death and the reasons she couldn't date him for their conversation to veer to his search for a new church home.

"What did you think of Hickory Ridge?"

"There's a lot to like." He paused to lower Max, who climbed into the station wagon and started flipping a bunch of switches on the dashboard. "Everyone seems so friendly. I could barely get past all of the people who wanted to shake hands so that I could catch up with you."

Brett knew the minute the words were out of his mouth that it was the wrong thing to have said. Did he have to come out and *announce* that he'd only visited Hickory Ridge because he wanted to see her? Tricia's sudden change in demeanor—now as tight and impenetrable as Rusty, Jr.'s—showed she hadn't missed his slip, either.

What he'd told her was technically true. He was searching for a new church. He just hadn't been working too hard at it. The faith community he'd grown up in—the one his parents still attended and the one he'd shared with Claire—didn't fit anymore. At least he hadn't let that part slip.

"The choir was good," he said, searching for anything to fill the space.

But Tricia didn't—maybe couldn't—play along by adding her own inane contribution. Suddenly, he wanted to do anything to make her relax again, even if it meant driving from this church parking lot and never returning. For her sake. Maybe he should just forget his plan to get to know her better, to become her friend.

A friend? He tried to ignore the voice inside him that suggested he shouldn't have been so appreciative of the way *a friend* looked in that long, flowery skirt and that prim but feminine blouse. Max saved Brett from berating himself over the lapse by honking the horn several times. Tricia shrugged apologetically and raced to the car door. He hated his ridiculous sense that she was running, not toward her child, but away from him.

He took the uncomfortable ache settling deep in his chest as his cue that it was time to cut his losses while they were still few and walk away. She clearly expected him to. And he would have obliged her, if a couple hadn't approached Tricia's station wagon.

A golden-haired woman reached out a hand to him. "It's Brett, isn't it? I'm Charity McKinley, and this is my husband, Rick."

Brett shook hands with them, but when he lifted an eyebrow over being recognized, Charity grinned. "I work with Jenny. She brought a picture of you to work one time."

He nodded. Oh, Jenny, the one who was proud enough of her brother to have his picture at work but too embarrassed by what he did for a living to let anyone know. His resentment over his sister's telling omission threatened to resurface, but then he never would have met Tricia Williams. He wished he could wish for that but he didn't. "Jenny's told me about you."

Charity chuckled. "Good, I hope."

"Most of it, anyway."

Rolling her eyes, Charity turned to Tricia, who came back from her car, a wiggling four-year-old under her arm. Rick McKinley stepped forward and took hold of Max, deftly tossing him over his shoulder to a chorus of the boy's giggles. Already, Tricia appeared more naturally colored and more animated than she'd looked since Brett had approached her.

Charity stepped to her husband's side to tickle Max. "We'll see you in a few minutes, right, Tricia?"

"We'll be there." After she said it, Tricia tossed a nervous glance toward Brett.

Charity must have intercepted the look, because she turned back to Brett. ''You'll join us for our little luncheon, too, of course. We'd love it.''

Tricia's eyes must have doubled in size, and Rusty, Jr. appeared on the verge of a choking fit.

''Ah.'' Brett stalled, searching for the excuse Tricia and her son so obviously wanted him to give. ''You know—''

''Please come,'' Lani crooned in that same cajoling tone she'd used that night at the bowling alley.

''Please, please,'' Max called out.

If Tricia had begged, ''Please, please don't come,'' Brett would have given in to her plea. He'd never been able to resist a woman's call for help. But she didn't ask. She just sat there with this neutral expression. So the only entreaty he had to respond to had come from the children. He couldn't deny them, either.

''Sounds great.''

Great? That was an optimistic term. *Excruciating.* Now that was probably more like it. Tricia would probably spend the whole time at lunch looking at him as if she wished he would disappear. He wondered why he'd given in so easily in the first place.

But after one glance at the lovely woman who was pointedly not looking back at him he had his answer. Was it the emptiness he sometimes caught in her gaze when she thought no one was watching? Was it that fierce independence that she used as a wall to shield herself from the likes of him?

No matter what it was, Brett felt this crazy need to

protect her, whether she liked it or not. One more time, he looked over at Tricia, and this time he caught her watching him. The way his heart drummed inside his chest, he couldn't call his interest in her just friendly. There was no doubt about it. He was in way over his head.

If this event was just lunch at the McKinleys' house, Brett wondered what a real party would have looked like there. Pink and purple helium balloons dotted the high ceiling, and colorful streamers crisscrossed the room. A huge banner with the words, "Welcome, Julia," stretched from one corner to the other.

The small living room was so crowded that no one had heard the doorbell when he rang or the door when he opened it. He recognized several faces from church that morning—the minister, the youth minister and his wife, and Hannah, of course—among those milling about the comfortable living room, but there were a few unfamiliar faces as well. He didn't know where the children were, but since Max hadn't torpedoed him with his head yet, he figured the younger set had been shipped somewhere else for the afternoon.

The thought crossed his mind to slip right back out, but he caught sight of Tricia passing through the kitchen, and he closed the door behind him.

An uncomfortable sensation struck deep in his gut. So strange. So unfamiliar. He had no idea what to do next. Brett was so used to acting on instinct—that and some rigid training—and neither had failed him. Not since he'd stopped living his life for other people.

Maybe he would just hang out on the periphery, his own oversize version of a wallflower, until Tricia noticed him and felt guilty enough to come up and talk to him. But he probably had a long wait ahead of him.

"Brett, you made it," Charity called out. "We're so glad you could come."

He hadn't noticed the blonde's approach, having been too busy willing someone else to come over to him. Still, he smiled at his hostess and indicated with his head toward the banner. "Who's Julia?"

Charity chuckled. "No one explained it to you? You probably thought you were just coming to lunch. This is a luncheon for my sister, Julia, who just moved to Milford."

Rick came up behind Charity and shook Brett's hand. "You'll have to forgive my wife. She gets a little too enthusiastic sometimes." He gestured with his hand toward a raven-haired woman near the banner. "That's Julia over there," he said as Charity moved on to other guests. "Can't you see the resemblance?"

Now that Rick had mentioned it, he could. Their faces were similar, though one was light-haired, the other dark. Julia was slightly more rounded than the willowy Charity, but they were clearly related.

"They're half-sisters," Rick said as if to explain the dichotomy. "She's also single."

Brett might have studied the two sisters' resemblance if he wasn't so distracted by another dark-haired woman who approached Julia and started a conversation with her. Funny how he couldn't focus on Julia's shiny, black hair and classic features when Tricia stood next to her. Tricia's porcelain beauty appeared sweet and vulnerable by comparison. Why was he so drawn to someone with so many complications when a lovely young woman with probably far fewer was standing right next to her?

He must have stared too long because Rick elbowed him in the ribs. "Here, I'll introduce you."

Before Brett could stop him, Rick trudged across the room, looking over his shoulder as if he expected him to follow. He found himself shaking hands with the woman who had every right to be the center of attention at her own party and wishing that the open smile Julia Sims directed toward him could have been on Tricia's lips instead.

But then Tricia did smile. And the expression she leveled at him—some mix between a grin and a laugh—could have eclipsed the sun. His breath caught in his throat, which was good since he probably would have said something stupid before he got control of himself. Something like, *How did you get so beautiful?* For a man who prided himself on total control of his emotions, he had all the firmness of an overcooked noodle.

"Charity doesn't do anything halfway, so she couldn't make an exception for her sister's welcome party." Tricia indicated with her arms the decorations and the side table already laden with food. "Brett, you picked a great day to visit. This will give you a better opportunity to get to know some of the people at Hickory Ridge."

"What did you do with the kids, sell them at auction?"

Tricia laughed, but it sounded forced, not sweet and natural, the way she'd sounded that night at the hockey game. On their one, nearly perfect date.

"No, they're here. Charity just hired Steffie Wilmington to corral them. They're watching a video in the basement." She beamed at him again. "That will give the adults a chance to talk."

It was all Brett could do not to demand to know what had caused her to do a one-eighty about him. She'd been avoiding him before, and now she sounded downright eager to be around him. He opened his mouth to ask, but she started talking first.

"Did Charity tell you Julia just got her teaching degree, and she's substituting in the Huron Valley Schools, hoping to get a permanent teaching job?"

So that's it. He was seething. How dare she try to pawn him off on some other woman as if he was a share of stock, available to the highest bidder. He ignored the voice inside that suggested she just thought he was a nice guy—though not for her—and wanted him to meet someone equally likeable.

"Julia, Brett is a Michigan State Police trooper."

Tricia's words drew his attention back to her. She'd

made a point of mentioning his career when she'd slipped on her imaginary matchmaker hat.

Julia turned to him. "What a great career. Do you like patrolling the roads?"

"I love it. How do you like teaching?"

"I love it, too. I just can't wait to get a long-term sub position or my own classroom. Well, I'd better…" Julia let her words trail off, and she shrugged shyly.

For her part, Julia seemed embarrassed about being blatantly pushed toward him, but she was trying to be polite. Even Rick wore a strange expression, though a few minutes before he'd made a point of saying that his sister-in-law was single. Perhaps Rick, too, wondered if Tricia was trying too hard to set Brett and Julia up.

He needed to get out of there now, while he had some dignity intact. Okay, it was a good thirty minutes too late for that. But a real man knew when he was beat, and this real man had been defeated before he'd even started. He glanced about the small circle one last time, past the woman everyone was pushing him toward to the one determined to push him away.

You're off the hook. He should have said the words to her, but he couldn't mouth them, not with her looking at him so nervously. But instead of feeling compassionate, this time her fears only annoyed him. They didn't give her the right to push him off on the first new woman who came into town. And he would have told her so if Charity hadn't returned from the kitchen right then.

"Hey, everyone, it's time to eat. Tricia, Hannah, Serena and Andrew, there's a place for the children to eat in the basement. Steffie's getting their plates ready, so you can just sit down and enjoy."

"Not sure I remember how to do that," Serena Westin said, earning a laugh from the other adults.

Rick approached Serena from behind and squeezed her shoulder. "Then we'd better remind you."

"Do you think Steffie will be able to handle feeding all six kids?" asked Andrew. "We can get Tessa and Seth's plates ready if that will help her."

Charity waved away the suggestion. "She'll be fine. She was flirting with Brendan Hicks while she was *listening* to today's sermon, so I know she's good at multitasking."

The crowd laughed again, louder this time.

At Rick's nod, Reverend Bob bowed his head, and the others gathered in a circle and joined hands. A gnawing ache settled in the pit of Brett's stomach. He remembered feeling part of a church community like this once, feeling one in the spirit as they seemed to be, but that was a long time ago.

"Oh, Lord, we celebrate You today and Your gifts of family and friendship," the minister began. "We thank You for sending Julia to our faith community and for giving Brett the chance to visit with us. And we thank You for the new beginnings You give us...."

The reverend must have said more, but Brett heard nothing after the part about new beginnings. Was Reverend Bob, too, trying to play matchmaker between him and Charity's sister? Couldn't these people recognize that he wasn't the least bit interested in the black-haired beauty? That he was only interested in—

No, that wasn't it. If it were true that he only had eyes for Tricia—which he'd just established it was not—then his eyes were pretty much useless. She refused to see any possibility in him.

Why he felt compelled to peek at her then, he didn't know, but neither could he resist. Across the circle from him, Tricia squeezed her eyes shut. She looked so vulnerable with her eyes closed. Already, she was so small and fragile, but without her fire-filled gaze she appeared even more in need of a champion. Part of him wanted to be that hero, protecting her from anyone who might hurt or frighten her.

Him maybe most of all.

But another part of him felt restless. He was even more determined to prove that she was wrong about him. That he wasn't some naive risk-taker like the man who'd made her a widow. It was what he'd set out to do in the first place, and he wasn't going anywhere until he did it.

Chapter Six

"How are your classes going?"

Reverend Bob's question from the end of the table startled Tricia so much she nearly knocked over her iced tea on Charity's pristine white tablecloth. She gripped the sweating glass to cool off one of her hands. Just how long had she been sitting there staring off into space, barely present while the other adult guests around the mahogany dining room table visited with Charity's younger half-sister?

"Pretty well," she finally answered, still bothered by the words Reverend Bob had said in his blessing. Had he been trying to tell her that she should consider a *new beginning* with Brett? Forcing herself not to look at the man in question, she cleared her throat and tried again. "Statistics is a pretty hard class, but I really like marketing."

"Are you still maintaining that 4.0?"

She shrugged. "Trying to, anyway. Graduation's a long way off since I'm only taking a few classes each semester."

Seated next to her, Hannah reached over to pat her arm. "But you're doing it, right? You'll finish."

Tricia glanced down at the ham, scalloped potatoes and asparagus she'd been spreading around to decorate her plate instead of eating. "We both will, but you'll beat me to graduation, attending full-time."

"Maybe," Hannah said, one side of her lips pulling up in a half grin. "I'm not feeling confident with finals coming up."

"I'm not looking forward to those, either."

Tricia stayed occupied answering Robert and Diana Lidstrom's questions about her job, even remembered to nod at the story Serena was telling about the day two-year-old Seth flooded the parsonage's upstairs bathroom. Still, she was relieved when the others became involved in conversations that didn't directly involve her. Dealing with social situations was hard enough when Brett Lancaster wasn't seated right next to her, talking to Julia on his other side.

Charity could have made the whole situation easier if she hadn't separated the children from the adults. With her kids there, Tricia could have kept busy pouring soft drinks they shouldn't have been drinking or reminding Max to chew with his mouth closed.

That method had worked well at recent church gatherings, allowing her to avoid anything other than light conversation with her friends. Of course, they were friends, and they would have listened if she were to share more, but she couldn't. Then someone might suspect that she wasn't okay and that her wounds had healed, but they were still there, as deep as ever.

Shoving those thoughts away and rearranging those piles on her plate, she caught snatches of the conversations around her. Not that one interested her any more than the others, but Brett did seem to be hanging on Julia's words about growing up in Indiana.

"Did I hear you say you would be subbing for the next week at Johnson Elementary?" she heard Brett ask Julia.

"Yes, for one of the fourth-grade classes." Julia tilted her head in, a sign that she was listening attentively to him. "Do you know that school?"

"I occasionally do visits on behalf of the Brighton Post for the area schools' health and safety projects— when our community service officer lets me. I'm going to Johnson later this week."

Why hadn't Brett ever mentioned to her that he volunteered in the schools, or that he was visiting her children's school this week? She didn't want to acknowledge the unsettling feeling inside her as jealousy, but she was having a hard time defining it, and she was bothered that he'd informed Julia first. Julia, the sweet-tempered young woman she'd pushed his way not thirty minutes before. He sure worked fast, as much fun as Charity's sister seemed to be having sitting next to him.

As if Julia had sensed that unkind thought, she

leaned in and indicated to Tricia with a gesture of her hand. "Tricia's children attend Johnson."

"I didn't know that." Brett turned his head toward Tricia, his unwavering gaze making her face feel warm. Rick and Charity probably kept their thermostat too warm for this time of year.

Julia continued as if she didn't recognize how stifling the room had become. "I've subbed in Mrs. Gerrig's second grade, and Lani's in that one. Hopefully, I'll get to visit Rusty's first-grade class soon."

A breath caught in Tricia's throat at Julia's reference to her son by his first name alone. Church members had rarely referred to Rusty, Jr. by just the Christian name he shared with his father, even before. Now they never did.

Brett made a strange sound in his throat, as if he, too, recognized the newcomer's innocent mistake, but he didn't look away from Tricia. "I'll be speaking to some of the first-grade classes."

Tricia shifted in her chair. Rusty, Jr. had been enough of a problem after Brett had agreed to come to Rick and Charity's luncheon. She could just imagine what the boy would say after he met up with Brett again at school. Even more, she worried that her son would have a meltdown in his classroom, as volatile as his behavior had been lately.

"How do you find time in your work schedule to visit the schools?" Tricia asked, figuring she was expected to contribute to the conversation.

"It will be on my day off."

"How wonderful that you take time on your day off to work with children," Julia gushed.

Maybe she hadn't really gushed, but it had sounded like it when the younger woman said exactly what Tricia had been tempted to say herself, but hadn't because it sounded too much like gushing. Still, Tricia was having an awfully hard time reconciling this man—this hockey fan, this churchgoing man who gave bowling tips and extra hugs to her children, this community volunteer—to the man who carried a side-arm and risked his life every day he went to work.

Brett pushed away the compliment with a wave of his hand. "I enjoy doing it. I remember how cool I thought cops were when I was a kid."

Somehow before Julia leaped in with a comment about how cool cops were now, again giving voice to Tricia's own secret thoughts, Rick stood at the end of the table and tapped a spoon on his water glass.

"Hey, listen to that sound." Rick did it again for effect, definitely not the type of guy used to giving toasts or making announcements using crystal. "Maybe I should start a band."

"And maybe I should have married a grown-up," Charity chimed from beside him as she came to her feet.

Rick tossed her an exasperated look that turned into a grin. "Anyway, on behalf of my *darling* wife and myself, I would like to welcome her younger sister, Julia, to Milford. Who knew two years ago when we discovered Charity had a sister, that now we'd be inviting her into our home—temporarily, mind you.'' He winked at Julia, who smiled back at him.

The small crowd applauded, and Julia nodded to accept their welcome. No one mentioned that Charity had discovered Julia's existence on the same day she learned her father was very much alive and her mother had lied to her all her life. That Charity's mother, Laura Sims, was conspicuously absent from the day's festivities, showed the rift between mother and daughter needed more time to heal.

Julia stood, smiling at each individual before speaking. ''Thanks, everyone, for giving me such a warm welcome. You've all been so nice. My dad would have been happy to know I ended up here with Charity and at Hickory Ridge Community Church.''

All of the guests smiled back at her, but no one spoke. A few had unspent tears shining in their eyes. Everyone but Brett knew the bittersweet story of Charity finally meeting her father, only to lose him to a heart attack a year later.

Rick cleared his throat when Julia sat back down. ''Now, on to other things. You all know we've been discussing new programs for the church's Family Life Center ever since its construction was completed.''

''You mean since you finished building it, so you could host your wedding there?'' Andrew chimed.

Rick, the owner of R and J Construction and the general contractor on the building, grinned. ''Yes, since then. Anyway, Charity and I are finally going to get the new Christian singles group rolling on Tuesday night, and we need everyone to come and support it.''

"Does that mean I can come?" Robert asked, raising an eyebrow at his wife.

Diana poked him in his middle-aged paunch. "Only if you plan to sleep on the couch Tuesday night.''

Rick shot up a puff of air into his hair. "I meant those of you who are single. Six of us here are married. Six are single. And Charity and I get to go, anyway, since we're heading up Faith Singles United.''

"So we expect to see you six there," Charity added.

Several voices erupted at once as everyone tried to make excuses not to attend, but Charity shook her head and waved away their attempts. "We're not going to be drawing numbers and pairing you off. It's just a fun night out—with food and sporting activities—for people who have in common that they are single.''

"That's not something for us old fogies," Mary Nelson, Hannah's child care provider, pointed out.

Reverend Bob gestured toward her with his hand and nodded his agreement.

Rick shook his head. "Mary, as if you could be called an old fogy, anyway. If there were such a thing as the fountain of youth, you'd be using it for a birdbath in your front yard." He nodded for his wife to continue their sales pitch.

"'Christian Singles United' is for all singles—divorced and widowed as well as never-marrieds.''

Charity pointed at the minister. "You said that yourself when we were discussing it."

"As much as I'd love to come," Hannah said with a long pause, "with my studies and with Mary obviously unavailable to sit, I won't have any child care."

"Me, neither," Tricia added, relieved to have an excuse. Anyway, she had decided in the last few weeks that she wasn't ready to date, and she should turn down all of her friends' future attempts to set her up on blind dates. The last one was a disaster.

"That's where Robert and I come in," Diana announced, before turning back to her surprised husband. "Didn't I mention, sweetheart, that we'd be staffing the child care rooms, with help from the teens in the youth department?" She took in his frown. "Guess not."

Charity glanced around the table again. "Does that cover everyone's excuses?"

Andrew lifted Serena's left hand to show her wedding ring. "We're not single."

"Okay, you're excused."

Brett raised his hand. "I'm not a member of this church."

But Charity pounced on that. "You're still invited. This program will be a community ministry where we can reach Christian singles from various churches as well as those who don't have a church home."

She might as well have said *like you, Brett,* as clearly as she implied it.

"Okay, does that cover everyone?" Rick asked,

glancing at Julia, the only single person in the room who hadn't made an excuse.

But she only shrugged. "Sounds like fun. I'm new here. It will be a good chance to meet some new people."

Why did that comment bug Tricia so much? Of course, Julia was new to the community and would benefit from meeting some new friends. Of course, she was single and never married and might have the opportunity to meet someone she could fall in love with. So why did Tricia get the sense that the only reason the new young woman might want to attend a volleyball event in a sweaty gymnasium was the possibility that Brett might be there?

That only brought up more questions in Tricia's mind. When had she become so mean-spirited that she would question other people's motives? Beyond that, even if Julia were only coming because Brett might be there, why should she care? She'd tried to push the two of them together herself.

None of this should matter to her. She had no claim on Brett. And she didn't even want to have one. At least that was what she kept telling herself. Why was that thought beginning to sound flat, even in her own ears?

Charity stretched her hands wide in a sweeping gesture. "Great, we'll count on all of you. We were worried this first event might have low attendance. We've already had it listed in the newspaper community calendars, but we were still worried. Now we know that at least all of you will be there.''

Tricia expelled a sigh as quietly as she could. She would have to grin and bear this one event. That didn't mean she would have to come every first and third Tuesday of each month, the regular meeting times for this group. Thinking about attending made her tired, and when she glanced at Brett, he drew his eyebrows together in a curious expression, as if he couldn't understand her weariness. No one else could, so why should he?

Because the conversation had died off, Charity started clearing away the dishes, and everyone pitched in to help. Just as Charity clicked the dishwasher shut, the door to the basement burst open, and a slew of children poured up the stairs, an overwhelmed-looking sixteen-year-old girl chasing after them.

''Mommy, Rusty, Jr. punched me in the belly,'' Max announced when he stood in front of Tricia.

''Yeah, so look where he bit me.'' And sure enough, Rusty, Jr. produced an arm with a red spot shaped just like a set of primary teeth.

''He started it,'' Max countered.

Tricia crouched to handle the crisis when Brett stepped up to the boys and into the center of the fray.

''Whoa, guys,'' he said with laughter in his voice. ''What happened here? Are there more casualties in the basement?''

''Not anymore,'' Lani said, showing off a hand-shaped slap mark on her forearm.

"Let's see if we can work this out," Brett said.

Before Tricia could warn him he was making a mistake, Brett rested a hand on each of the boys' shoulders, the way their father used to do. Max would never have remembered. But Rusty, Jr. probably could never forget.

Immediately, the older boy jerked his shoulder away from Brett's hand and turned on him. "Don't touch me. Don't you ever touch me again!" His voice grew louder with each word until it was a shriek.

His face appearing carefully blank, Brett released Max's shoulder, too, and held his hands in a soft surrender pose. "I'm sorry I touched you. I just wanted to help."

"You can't help. Nobody can help!" Rusty, Jr. yelled again, backing away until he bumped into Reverend Bob.

The minister lowered his hands as if to hug Rusty, Jr. but then stopped himself as the child stiffened. "Young man, why don't we go on a walk so we can talk some? Maybe we all need some fresh air."

Rusty, Jr. looked up at the minister with wide eyes, as if noticing for the first time the crowd of adults witnessing his meltdown. Still, he shook his head stubbornly before turning to stare at a kitchen wall.

The room was as quiet as any space could be, with twelve adults and six children either crowding inside or craning their necks through the doorway to catch a glimpse of the melee. Whispers bounced off the walls, becoming strange slurring sounds.

Humiliation blanketed Tricia, who rolled her lips inward and tried to calm the fury roiling just beneath it. She'd never been so ashamed of one of her children.

She glanced across the room and caught Brett's gaze and hoped he could see how sorry she was. He only smiled. Obviously, he was used to dealing with domestic disputes, maybe even those involving weapons. He nodded his head in what she could only sense was a signal of encouragement, as if he believed she could handle this, possibly even that he was there to help her if she couldn't.

That assurance made her relax inside, that is until the boy turned to face them, looking back and forth between Tricia and the police officer. Then Rusty, Jr. pinned his mother alone with his stare.

"Mom, tell him we don't need him. Tell him we don't need anybody!"

Chapter Seven

The orange cast of daybreak was bleeding into the eastern sky Tuesday as Brett drove along Stobart Road and the southernmost border of General Motors Proving Grounds. At least part of the automaker's sprawling test facility was in Livingston County and in his regular patrol area.

He tried to tell himself that he was only going to Milford, in Oakland County, because it had the closest Starbucks, and he needed the caffeine. It had nothing to do with the fact that Tricia Williams lived and worked right in the village.

Lying to himself was getting old. Still, he wasn't ready to give up the habit, so he stopped at the downtown shop to quell his java need before popping in to Kroger to get bottled water. And to see if she was working.

He found her behind the deli counter, shaving

smoked turkey breast for the first in a line of custom-ers. Busy or not, he couldn't believe she didn't notice him at first, since he stuck out like a huge blueberry on a white tile floor in his uniform amid the bright grocery store aisles. But the fact that she didn't notice gave him time to study her, to admire the fluid way she moved from task to task, like a dancer in a hairnet and food service gloves. She wore a smile on her face, not the frown of someone who didn't enjoy her work. He liked knowing she was happy doing her job, though she worked out of necessity.

"May I help who's next?" The words were already out of her mouth before she looked up at him, but when she did, she jerked her head. "Oh…hi. Is there something I can get you, Officer? Or should I say Trooper Lancaster?"

"No, Brett's fine," he said, though he should have asked her to address him formally when he was in public. He didn't like his subconscious suggestion that he'd like her to address him even more personally than that. He hated admitting that from the start he'd wanted something more than friendship from her. That had been his first mistake. His standing here gaping at her like a lovelorn teenager was just one in a long string of blunders concerning her.

"What are you doing in Milford?"

She became quiet for a several seconds, scanning his uniform from hat to shoes. Of course, she'd never seen him in uniform before. He'd grown accustomed to the odd stares, the surreptitious glances and even the disdainful looks that usually came from teenage boys in convenience stores, but it was different being under her scrutiny. It was somehow critical that he pass her inspection. He wished he could see whatever she saw.

Her eyes widened as she studied him, and she hesitated as her gaze landed on the silver badge pinned to his uniform. Wary. That was the only way he could describe her expression as she looked at him. She must have realized she was staring, because she averted her eyes.

"I'm required to wear a bulletproof vest under my uniform."

Why had he told her that? Because he wanted her to know he took precautions against getting himself killed at work? Well, it didn't take a rocket scientist to realize that a trooper whose heart was carefully guarded behind bullet-stopping Kevlar could get just as dead when some dirtbag shot him in the head.

A touch of pink danced on her cheeks, whether over his referring to what was beneath his shirt or her getting caught watching too long, he wasn't sure. But the corners of her mouth turned up. "I'm glad you wear one," she said finally.

At least she hadn't suggested he skip wearing the vest for a few days to increase the chances that he wouldn't be around long and would stop stalking her.

Tricia cleared her throat as the moment became more awkward. "I thought you patrolled Livingston County."

"Mostly. But I needed a Starbucks coffee."

She glanced down at his hands, where he held a six-pack of bottled water. "And water?"

That and to see her, but he didn't figure he needed to tell her that. Her eyes narrowed, signaling she'd figured it out anyway. "Don't worry, the post knows exactly where I am with GPS—that's a global positioning system—in the car." Sometimes he hated having someone constantly know where to find him, but he had to deal with it.

As if on cue, he heard a beep and then a murmur of voices on his radio, attached at his shoulder. He listened to the communication from central dispatch and heard another agency get the bid to respond to a car fire.

When he looked up again, Tricia was already handing a bag of colby-jack cheese to a hunched woman who had approached the counter.

Tricia cleared her throat when they were alone again. "Well, I'd better…"

Brett recognized that as Tricia's departing comment even before a stern-faced woman appeared from some food preparation room behind the deli area. Tricia's guilty expression when she saw the woman, who wore a supervisor's badge, reminded him of a suspect caught with a nickel bag of grass and several pieces of drug paraphernalia riding shotgun in his front seat. As if Tricia had been doing something wrong by talking to him.

The supervisor's face softened instead of turning

more steel-like. "Hey Tricia, why don't you take your break now?"

Brett could have kissed the woman, right on the straight line that formed her lips, for foiling Tricia's attempt to push him away again. What kind of man kept pursuing a woman who kept rejecting him? His kind apparently, but he wasn't in the mood to dissect his messed-up psyche.

Tricia opened her mouth as if to argue but then closed it and stepped from behind the glass deli case. "It's been nice seeing you," she said as she passed him.

But he wasn't going to let her get off that easily and waste the gift of time from her boss, so he caught up with her before she reached the bakery department. "Hey, I'm sorry about Sunday with Rusty, Jr."

"Yeah, me, too."

He matched her step for step as she kept walking, like some ridiculous slow-speed police chase, until she stopped in front of the self-serve bakery cases. When he was convinced she wouldn't say another word to him, she shook her head slowly and then glanced over her shoulder.

"I don't know what's gotten into him lately. I thought the grief counselor was making some headway with him, and then he does something like that."

Brett kept his face blank. Was the seemingly invincible Mrs. Williams finally admitting she didn't have a superhero emblem emblazoned on some imaginary leotard beneath her work uniform? The near-admission that she couldn't handle every situation with her own sheer strength must have been killing her. On reflex, he reached out a hand to touch her shoulder, but he halted the movement in mid-air and tucked his hand in his pocket.

"I shouldn't have intervened. It wasn't like I was on duty or something."

She turned to face him. "You probably have more experience dealing with situations like that than I have. I'd just never seen my son like that before."

"It could have been a fluke. Nothing to worry about."

But it hadn't felt like a fluke. The boy's fury had been palpable. It had been a cry for help. So why was he trying to allay his mother's fears instead of telling her what he really thought? Maybe it was the desperation so evident in Tricia's eyes. In his work, he'd seen that same type of desperation in other mothers—women whose children were close to the edge...or over it.

"I hope you're right."

Her grateful smile and her suddenly shiny eyes made him regret more that he'd oversimplified the situation. Admittedly, the family's case was minor compared to the many sad stories he'd learned of other troubled children. Rusty, Jr. was just a sad little boy, and who could blame him when his father had been ripped away?

Unlike the other cases, when Brett had suggested agencies where the mothers could go for help and had even followed up to ensure they found it, this time he wanted to do more. He wanted to *be* that help. But Tricia wasn't asking for him to be her hero, so why was he continually donning his cape?

For several seconds Tricia stood, staring across the displays of baked goods, likely seeing something far different from raisin bread and bagels. "He's met every man I've gone out with in the last year. He's never acted like that to any one of them...except you."

Because it's different this time, he wanted to shout at her. He'd recognized it. Obviously, Rusty, Jr. had, too, from the first night when he'd caught Tricia and Brett watching each other. Lani probably knew it, too, as little got past that sharp child. Max still lived in a four-year-old's oblivion. So what was Tricia's excuse?

This situation had to be different because Tricia had never been attracted to any of the other men she'd allowed friends to set her up with. And she'd never agreed to a second date with any of them.

But she *had* agreed to go out with Brett again, even if that date never happened. She would have gone, too, if only he'd been a butcher, or a used-car salesman or a driver of a big rig. He resisted the temptation to feel frustrated over that fact again. He was who he was, and she would just have to accept it.

Or not.

"Are you going tonight?" he blurted over his misgivings.

"Going where?" she asked unnecessarily as she

shook open a pastry bag. "Oh, you mean the singles' group at church? I don't think so. I have a lot of studying to do, and I can't get child care."

"Didn't Robert and Diana say that they—"

"Oh, that's right—they'll have child care." She opened the glass door and used tongs to collect a muffin. "You know, I don't really feel comfortable at singles things. You hinted at it yourself from just the number of first dates I've had. I'm not ready to date."

Brett's insides jerked, so he had to force himself to relax, much the same way he did when he approached a potentially explosive scene. And like some of those times, this one would require fancy verbal sparring.

"Didn't Charity say it was just going to be some laid-back team sports and food with a bunch of other people, who all just happen to be single, like you?"

"They're not like me."

She had him there. Most singles who attended probably wouldn't be young widows who had lost their spouses to stupid accidents. He also doubted that any of the women would be as mesmerizing or as intelligent as Tricia.

Nor could any be as stubborn.

Okay, he was posting a losing score in this conversation—thirty-love, he figured, were the game tennis—so he put his best effort behind his next serve.

"You don't want to disappoint Rick and Charity, do you? Especially when they're trying so hard to establish this new ministry." When she turned to study the doughnut display, he knew he had her. Maybe it was unfair for him to play on her sense of obligation to her friends, but she hadn't played fair since he'd known her. She'd judged him without even knowing him, and she'd tried to push him at another woman who, no matter how lovely, could never be the person he wanted. Her.

"I don't know."

"Of course, you do. And you want to go. I can tell." Her body language, crossing her arms protectively and avoiding eye contact, suggested she wasn't *open* to anything, but he had to give it a shot.

"You're right," she conceded. "Rick and Charity would be pretty disappointed if I didn't come." She turned and walked toward the checkouts.

Brett glanced to see if anyone was watching and then flexed his arm toward his body in the classic "ch-ching" gesture. And he was tuning up inside for a very bad rendition of Handel's "Hallelujah" chorus, when Tricia stopped in the aisle ahead of him and approached again.

"I'm glad you talked me into this. Rick and Charity will be happy to see me out. They worry about me sometimes." She paused until he met her gaze again. "Did I tell you that Rick was Rusty's best friend?"

"No, you didn't," he replied.

"Oh, well. I'll see you tonight then." She waved and then popped into a checkout line, not looking back at him.

Rusty's best friend. He had to give Tricia credit. She'd planned her counterattack and had carefully executed it, just as he'd planned his arguments for convincing her to go. He didn't want to ponder why it mattered so much that she be there, even if she'd likely ignore him or push more single women his way. The question chased him as he purchased bottled water he didn't want and headed back out to the coffee—cold now—in his patrol car. Already, dark clouds had encroached upon the sunny morning, turning the sky to an orangey-gray and promising to deliver upon the predicted scattered thunderstorms.

As he drove out of Milford, taking the freeway this time back into Livingston County, he tried to focus only on the asphalt ribbon and the drivers swishing past each other on their way to the important destinations of their lives. But his thoughts kept returning to the evening's plans and how they might affect his own life.

He'd been invited to the Christian Singles United kickoff, but he was under no obligation to attend. He wouldn't have gone, either, if Tricia had refused to go. At least he could admit that much to himself. But he was going. In fact, this would be the second church-related event, outside services, he'd attended in one week.

That this was Tricia's church had a good deal to do with why he'd accepted the invitations, but was there more to his sudden interest in spending time with a church group? He hadn't spent this much time in a church community since he and Claire had split up. His faith and Christian service were so inextricably tied to Claire that he wondered sometimes if he'd had any faith separate from her. He wanted to believe he did.

Why all of a sudden was he imagining himself and Tricia together, doing some beneficial work for God? Hadn't he learned his lesson the first time he'd allowed faith and a relationship with a woman to mix? No, he never wanted to feel that way again, as if his Christian walk had been sliced off just below the knees, leaving him kneeling but without a prayer.

The pain. He needed to focus on it, to allow himself to feel it again, though he'd promised himself he wouldn't go there anymore. It was like returning home after the old homestead had burned to the ground. None of that pain was worth reliving, except here he was, setting himself up to be eviscerated again.

It would be different this time. The side of his mouth pulled up into a smirk at these famous last words. Obviously, he'd already lost the edge, if he believed that. Already, there was proof in that he couldn't resist the way Tricia drew him to her, tempting him to take care of her, no matter how much she denied needing or wanting anyone.

He couldn't afford to let anyone inside again. Relying on someone was dangerous for him. He'd barely survived the last time. If he had any sense at all, he would never take the risk again.

The rain that started pelting the windshield ripped him from his confusing thoughts, providing what he recognized as only temporary relief. He would see Tricia tonight, and those unacceptable thoughts of anything beyond a casual friendship would return to taunt him.

Outside his car, idiots continued to whiz by as if they believed they could stop when cars in front of them hit their brakes. Experience told him the rest of his shift would be a busy one, so he didn't even blink when the call came across the radio from central dispatch.

Within seconds, he was speeding through traffic with his overhead light flashing and his siren blaring. For everyone's sake, he hoped no one would hit their brakes in front of him. His windshield wipers flapped with futile strokes and he raced past drivers, most of whom had obeyed the law and granted him right-of-way.

As he came upon the scene of the three-vehicle accident, taking to the shoulder to navigate past the cars already backing up, the knot that he'd come to know as a police-work sixth sense formed inside his gut. He observed the too-flat roof of the blue sedan that had rolled, and he started scanning for bodies.

Having beaten him to the scene by a few seconds, Trooper Joe Rossetti, who had parked his cruiser on the shoulder of the northbound lane, rushed to the upside-down blue sedan where other drivers and Good Samaritans were gathering.

Brett threw his raincoat over his uniform and the cover over his garrison cap and hurried to the nearest car, a sport-utility vehicle with a bashed front end and a crushed front-quarter panel. Its driver's side door hung open, hinting that whoever had been inside was healthy enough to have gotten out.

Barely pausing, he raced to the next closest vehicle, an older station wagon which, like the other, had no driver. The front was folded in like an accordion, and the rear-quarter panel didn't look much better. Infant car seat in the back. Still secured but empty. Windshield and passenger-side windows crushed.

Blood.

Ignoring the anxiety clenching the back of his throat, he scanned the grassy median. Where was the driver? The infant car seat, he hoped, had been empty all along, its usual occupant playing safely at day care. *Lord, let it be,* he prayed, despite the sinking feeling that his prayer was an hour too late.

Just as the first fire truck and ambulance arrived at the scene, Brett glanced into the grassy area across the southbound lane, and he saw them. At a run, he came upon a scene that, like a handful of others, he would never forget if he was a trooper for thirty years.

Slowly so as not to startle her, Brett approached the woman who sat statue-still in the tall grass, her body soaked with rain and blood. She had a few lacerations on her forearms and her face, but most of the blood had likely come from the crumpled, lifeless toddler in her arms.

"He's dead. My baby's dead." Her voice held no emotion, just the monotone of shock.

Brett nodded. "Ma'am, I'm Trooper Lancaster from

the Michigan State Police. I'm just checking for your son's pulse, okay?'' He crouched low, slipped on a rubber glove and pressed his fingertips to the child's carotid artery, confirming what he already knew.

"He kept unbuckling his car seat," the woman said, seeming to speak more to herself than him. "We were going to get one he couldn't undo."

He nodded again to acknowledge her moot point. He'd seen a lot of would haves, could haves and should haves in this job.

A pair of emergency workers rushed to them, so Brett could move a few steps away and radio in.

"It's a 'k,'" he spoke into his radio, using the lingo for "killed." "Send out the ME."

The medical examiner's services would be required at this scene along with the Jaws of Life to extract the driver from the blue sedan, and a Detroit emergency helicopter in case the guy made it. Brett needed to fill out accident reports from the other driver who had only minor injuries and would be treated at the scene.

He wanted to stay busy to keep his mind off Tricia and hopeless causes in general, but he would never wish for a scene like this one in a million years. If he could choose the way life went, he would never have to see that kind of pain in a mother's eyes again.

But he would see it; that much he knew. He could count on one hand the number of things he'd had control over in his lifetime, testing for the state police being one of them. But another one of those rare things would be happening tonight at a small community church in Milford.

Would he listen to his self-preservation instinct, or would he take the chance on really getting to know someone who just might become the most important person in his life? Was he living or only existing? Just as he'd taken a little longer than the average person to become what he wanted to be when he grew up, maybe it had taken him longer to figure out how to live as well. Maybe he was ready now.

He would take a chance with Tricia tonight, for better or worse. At least then, unlike the woman whose loss of that spirited child would haunt her, he would never have to wonder what might have been.

Chapter Eight

Tricia knew the moment she dropped off the children in one of the classrooms in Hickory Ridge's Family Life Center that night, purposely a half hour late, that it had been a mistake to come at all. Not that she hadn't been having misgivings about attending Faith Singles United all day, since Brett had walked out of the grocery store.

Part of it had to have been seeing him in that uniform. Her pulse had tripped, and she'd had to bite back a gasp when she'd seen him on the other side of the display case, appearing taller and more formidable than the man who'd taught her about hockey and played with her children.

Command-bearing—that was the only way she could describe his deep blue uniform and hat. More than that, it was the way he wore the uniform, his shoulders tight against the seams and his chest pressing full behind the silver badge on one side and the silver bar bearing his name on the other side. Though he seemed like a different person than the one she'd come to know in jeans and khakis, this look suited him as well. It just fit. She suspected that the job matched him just as perfectly. A good man in a career where he could do the world good.

For a few seconds, she'd wished she was someone else, someone who could appreciate the many gifts a man like Trooper Brett Lancaster could bring to her life. Maybe someone like Julia. Her sudden jealousy over Julia's freedom and opportunity had made Tricia more uncomfortable than even Brett's presence in her store had.

She'd sensed her co-workers' gazes upon them as they'd crossed the aisles to the bakery department and again to the checkout. Later, she'd endured dozen of questions about her being a suspect in a murder investigation or, worse yet, dating a cop. Her explanations about them being just friends had sounded flat, even to her ears. That had bothered her even more.

So why was she standing there in the doorway to the gymnasium, knowing full well that she shouldn't have come? Her attendance gave the wrong message to her friends—that she was interested in dating. Now fellow church members would probably continue setting her up with the few remaining single Christian men in southeast Michigan.

Worse than that, her being there might encourage one man in particular to think there was a chance for something more than friendship between them. In fairness to him, Brett had never asked for more than her friendship, and she was beginning to think she could use a few more friends.

Ignoring the tingle that scaled her spine, Tricia stood gripping the frame of the propped-open metal door separating the gym from the rest of the building. Inside a crowd of about twenty adults gathered, the greater portion divided into two teams at a volleyball net. Mostly their performance was a comedy of net serves, missed sets and hopeless spikes, but the players appeared to be having a blast anyway. And they provided entertainment for the half-dozen stragglers on the sidelines, who were cheering on both teams equally.

Some Hickory Ridge members were among the players as were a few of Tricia's customers from the grocery store. At least a third, though, had unfamiliar faces, meaning that Rick and Charity's publicity efforts had been successful. The mix was good, too, with as many blondes, brunettes and redheads as silver-haired guests and those with receding hairlines.

Still, the event resembled a lineup of choices not unlike the deli case at work. Only this one had no glass. The whole idea of it disturbed her. Three older women on the sidelines were watching Reverend Bob, each smiling a little brighter in hopes of garnering his attention. Hannah wasn't doing so badly herself, with two friendly-looking young men trying their best to make her laugh.

These people were only searching for companionship among other Christians, and maybe the opportunity to meet the person God had planned for them. What was so wrong with that? The fact that none of it seemed right to her was just another sign that she shouldn't have come.

For a few seconds longer, Tricia scanned the crowd, surprised by the pang of disappointment that struck her. Had she been looking for Brett in that small crowd? It didn't make sense. She didn't need him. Or anyone else.

Tricia backed away from the door, her pulse racing, her palms damp. Was he the only reason she'd come? And if he was, then why hadn't she had the good sense just to stay home? Brett wasn't a good choice for her, and she knew it. So why couldn't she get him out of her mind?

She glanced out at the healthy-sized crowd again. Rick and Charity didn't need her there to fill space when there were this many people attending. Already making up an excuse for when she picked up the children five minutes after she'd left them, Tricia took a second step backward. She would have turned to make her escape, but she backed into something solid, and whatever—rather *whoever*—she'd struck let out a grunt on impact. Still, two strong hands came to rest on her upper arms, likely to steady her though they accomplished just the opposite.

After absorbing that shocking touch and inhaling a woodsy scent she would have recognized anywhere, she didn't need him to speak for her to guess his identity. But her nerve endings danced when he did, especially on her neck where his breath skimmed across her skin.

"Did you just get here, too?"

Tricia whirled to face him, wishing her cheeks would stop burning. "Yes." *And I shouldn't have come at all.*

He hooked his thumbs through the belt loops of very faded jeans. "I had to work overtime so I thought I'd be the last one to show up."

Brett had a rushed look about him, and his short hair still looked damp from a recent shower.

"Still looks like you are the latest," she answered, indicating with her head that he was still behind her.

"You're right, unless some real straggler comes along." He kindly didn't mention that she'd been backing out the door, although it would have been obvious to anyone that she'd been about to bail. "Are you going in?"

"Might as well."

Brett followed her out onto the glossy gym floor. "At least there's food."

"And people," she added as several turned to wave or to watch them cross the floor. None made her as nervous as the man beside her, with plenty of space between them but still close enough that she sensed his nearness.

They must have caught sight of Julia Sims at the

same time because when Tricia turned to face him he was turning back to her.

"Look who's here—"

"Don't."

His curt answer startled her, but she tried not to let it show. "What?"

"Don't push Julia at me again. I had quite enough of that on Sunday—from you and from Rick."

"But she's perfect. She's young, educated, never married—"

"Not interested. Really." Although his voice had taken on a hard edge, he chuckled. "Look, I just don't want to be set up again. Not with anybody."

"But she—"

Brett interrupted her with a shake of his head. "Remember, my last setup didn't go so well. I'd just as soon get my own dates—and my own friends—if that's all right with you."

He'd tossed in that part about friends for her benefit, and she knew it. That was all he'd asked of her, and still she'd pushed him away.

She shrugged. "Fine."

"Good, now that that's settled, let's get something to eat. I'm starving."

But there was no spring to his step as he crossed the floor toward the table laden with snacks. Come to think of it, Brett didn't seem to have his usual energy and intensity. Even his eyes lacked their normal sparkling light that always made her smile. Strangely, he looked like someone who needed a friend tonight.

Then she remembered. There'd been something on the radio news about a big accident with fatalities on M-23 that had closed the southbound lanes for several hours. Had Brett worked the accident?

Grabbing a paper plate, she moved beside him at the food table, surveying the bounty of cut vegetables, fruit, cookies and frosted brownies before putting a few on her plate. Brett had said he was starving, but his plate was nearly empty except for one brownie and two carrot sticks.

"Bad day at the office?" she asked when she stopped by him at the end of the table.

His answer was a stark expression. He might have said more, but the volleyball game broke up then, and the crowd descended upon them. Reverend Bob was the first to reach them, a paper cup of punch already clasped in his hand.

"Tricia, we were beginning to wonder if you were going to make it." The minister took a long drink from his cup and pushed his salt-and-pepper hair back from his forehead. "I'm glad you did. You, too, Brett. It's good seeing you again." He gripped the younger man's hand.

Rick approached from behind them and wrapped an arm around Tricia's shoulder. "Hey, you made it. Should we be impressed that you *both* were fashionably late?"

Tricia didn't miss the way Rick stressed the word "both" like the protective older brother he'd become for her ever since Rusty died. Brett couldn't have missed it, either, especially since she'd made a point of telling him about Rick's friendship with her late husband.

Soon they were surrounded by half a dozen Hickory Ridge members. Hannah didn't join the others, still hanging out by the volleyball net and deep in conversation with a handsome blond man. Tricia was glad the singles group was benefiting someone. Hannah deserved to meet someone nice.

Tricia tried to listen to the lively banter of some of her closest friends, but she felt distracted. Not by the prospective glances from a thirty-something gentleman across the gym, either. All she cared about was the strangest thing—the very thing she would never have thought she would have wanted. She needed to be alone with Brett Lancaster.

The parking lot was emptying and the safety lights had come on by the time Brett trudged out toward his car. Strange how he'd looked forward to the singles event but now couldn't wait to get away from it. He'd been in no shape to go, though seeing Tricia, no matter what his mood, had been worth it. Especially after she'd stopped throwing him at other women and had quit trying to avoid him.

"Brett, do you have a minute?"

Tricia's voice stopped him. Any other time he would have been thrilled to hear those words, but now he needed to get away from people, to be alone so he could carefully compartmentalize his thoughts about the day's difficult events. He had come tonight because he'd promised himself no regrets, and yet he'd been so stripped of emotion that he'd regretted coming. Still, he couldn't help turning toward the woman who, for the first time, had approached him.

"Sure, what's up?"

Instead of pausing and remaining at a careful distance from him, Tricia walked right up to him and rested a hand on his forearm. He stared at her hand, his skin warm where she'd touched him. When he looked at her face, backlit in the parking lot lights, compassion filled her eyes.

"Do you want to talk about it…about what happened at work?" She squeezed his arm and then released it, leaving a dull void behind where her soft hand had rested. "Can you talk about the accident?"

Brett drew in a sharp breath. "How did you know?"

"There was something about it on the news. It was your usual patrol area, so I just guessed."

His nod came with a heavy sigh. "A mother lost her son this morning. It was awful."

"That's what they said on the news." Her words were simply stated, but her eyes shone with unspent tears. A mother's tears.

Brett coughed awkwardly, his eyes burning with unmanly tears he wouldn't allow himself to cry. But feeling—he could never stop that.

"That has to be such a hard part of your job, investigating accidents and going to homes to tell someone their loved one is dead.''

His stomach squeezed. ''I've only given a few death notices each year, but I can remember every one I've ever given. And from today, I doubt I'll ever forget the look on that mother's face as she held her child in her arms.''

Twin tears escaped from the corners of Tricia's eyes, falling down her porcelain cheeks. Her compassion was for that mother, but it was also for him. It humbled him. How open her heart was for others though she'd experienced more than her share of pain.

With a shaky voice, she finally spoke. ''Do police officers ever become immune to it?''

He shook his head. ''Oh, I hope not. Because, you know what? I'm a human being. If I ever become immune to the loss of life, then I'll know it's a signal for me to get out. And I will.''

''You'll never become callous. I know it.''

Surprised, Brett met her gaze, and though her eyes still glistened, she smiled.

He lifted an eyebrow. ''How do you know that?''

''I know.''

Tricia didn't say how she knew, but Brett wanted to believe her anyway. ''Glad to hear you know me so well.''

She stiffened, making him wish he'd kept his mouth shut. But then she tilted her head to the side as if studying him.

"Will you be okay at work tomorrow? I don't know how you can bounce back that quickly."

"I can bounce back. I have to. But I don't have to be at work tomorrow. Remember, I told you I'm doing some volunteer work."

"Oh, yeah, at the school, right?" At his nod, she continued. "That reminds me, this is a school night, so I had better pick up the kids before Robert and Diana come hunting for me."

As she started to back away, Brett was surprised by his sudden need to stop her. Such a contrast to a few minutes before when he'd thought he needed to be alone. What he'd really needed was to be with Tricia, to receive a healthy dose of her compassion. And he didn't want the moment to end.

"Tricia, wait."

She startled before turning to face him again. "What is it?"

The uncertainty he'd witnessed in her eyes on earlier occasions had returned. She'd probably realized she'd trampled on that invisible boundary drawn around her, and she was trying to scramble back inside it. He wanted to slow her retreat just as desperately.

"It's just that…" He let his words trail off, trying to come up with any excuse to keep her with him longer.

"Are you sure you're okay?"

"Yeah." At least he would be after he'd had a good night's sleep.

"Is there anything I can do to help?"

There probably wasn't. He just had to work through some thoughts in his head, and he would be fine. But if she happened to want to help with his mental well-being, then who was he to stop her? "You could see me tomorrow."

Tricia chewed on her bottom lip. "That's not exactly what I meant."

"Oh, I'm not talking about a date. I just thought maybe you'd like to tag along, help me get through the day." He was pouring it on thick, but he couldn't seem to stop himself. From the tender look in her eyes, he could see she was softening, so he pushed it a step further. "And it couldn't hurt for you to be there if I have to speak to Rusty, Jr.'s class."

He knew he'd won long before she assented, but the victory felt empty. Did he want her to have to be coerced into being with him? Was that enough for him? Well, it would have to be this time.

"Can I pick you up at nine?" He waited for her nod before he asked, "Do you have someone to watch Max?"

"Mary Nelson, Hannah's child care provider, watches him sometimes on days when he doesn't have preschool and I have to work. I'm sure she'd help out."

"Good, then it's settled."

Tricia licked her lips and nodded again before going back inside. Well, he'd made good on his promise to himself after all. He would have no regrets from tonight. He'd taken a chance on developing a deeper friendship with Tricia, and enthusiastically or not, she had accepted. Was friendship all he wanted from her? No, he had to admit to himself that he wanted more. But for now he would have to settle for whatever she was ready to offer him. It would have to be enough.

"Are you a real live cop?" Tricia asked in a child-like voice late the next morning as she and Brett walked out of the brick school building to his car. "Do you have a gun and everything?"

Brett smirked at her and readjusted his hat. "At least the kids liked me."

"Whatever you say."

But the first-graders had liked him. All of them, including Rusty, Jr., once the six-year-old got over the shock of seeing Brett in his classroom wearing a police uniform. Brett had ended up speaking to all the first-grade classes, and Tricia had tagged along to all of the presentations, but she'd stayed outside and observed her son's class surreptitiously through the narrow window in the door.

Brett couldn't have been more of a hit if he'd put on a big red nose and renamed himself Bozo. The principal loved him. The teachers loved him. And she…was impressed by him. She had to at least admit that much. He'd held the children's rapt attention with his interesting stories, even after they'd gotten over their excitement about his uniform. With a first-grade attention span, that was more than impressive.

She glanced back at him as he opened the car door

for her. "I'll have to stop calling you Trooper Lancaster and start calling you the Pied Piper of Brighton."

"I wouldn't go that far. That one boy said he was bored and wanted to go out to recess."

Tricia waited for him to climb in on his side before she answered. "Every crowd has a heckler."

"I must have had more than my share then."

"And you did great, answering questions about how much money you made and whether you'd ever killed anybody."

He grinned at her and then checked for traffic as he pulled out of the parking lot. "I did consider using my handcuffs a time or two."

"Admit it, you were just great with them. You're always good with children." Tricia had to stop herself because she was beginning to gush. That was all she needed, to go on and on about the way he'd reached out to her children…and her.

"I like kids" was all he said.

"Are you going to wear your uniform all day?" Tricia blushed the minute the words were out of her mouth. It must have sounded as if she wanted him to *not* be wearing his uniform, or something even more inappropriate.

The way his lips turned up indicated he hadn't missed her slip, but he was kind enough not to mention it. "I brought something to change into in case—" He stopped, suddenly checking his mirrors and looking uncomfortable.

"In case I invited you to lunch?" she finished for him, chuckling that she hadn't been as nice as him in letting his slip pass. She didn't bother waiting for him to nod before she continued. "Hey, I have a great idea. Why don't we pick up Max, and we can all get some lunch?"

"It was nice of you to offer," he said, playing along, but he turned a brilliant smile on her when he stopped at the light at Milford and Commerce.

And her knees went weak.

She'd never been so happy to be sitting down. Neither spoke for the rest of the ride to Mary Nelson's house.

"We can make it another time if you're…um… busy," Brett said quietly as he parked the car.

He was doing it again. Tricia's thoughts flashed back to that hockey game not so long ago when he'd invited her on a second date. That time when she'd hesitated, he'd offered to let her off the hook, even before the scuffle in the arena and her discovery about him.

Again, he was bowing out like the gentleman he was. Funny, but this time she didn't need his gallant gesture. She didn't want to be alone. More than that, she didn't want *him* to be alone. She'd recognized it last night. He needed a friend to talk to. Maybe they both did.

"No, I'm not busy." A tremor raced through her belly after the words were out of her mouth. No matter how small, she'd just taken a step out of her safety zone, away from the comfortably familiar place where she'd been hiding. There was no turning back now. "Today's a good day to have lunch."

Chapter Nine

It couldn't have been a more perfect day, Brett thought as he stretched out on a blanket in Tricia's backyard, with Max's abandoned action figures crowded around him. Content, he reached for his take-out bag and took the final bite of Tricia's Coney dog.

At the sound of the storm door clicking closed, he glanced up. Tricia, dressed like him in jeans and a sweatshirt, had tied a second sweatshirt over her shoulders. Okay, it wasn't quite picnic weather yet, but he didn't care.

She handed him one of the two cans of pop she'd carried out and then waved her free index finger in front of him. "You're going to regret eating that. You already ate two of your own."

"Wouldn't want to waste food."

Sitting a careful distance from him on the blanket, she grabbed the bags and checked the contents. Not a

French fry, a piece of bun or any chili sauce remained. "You're a member of the clean plate…er…bag club."

"Did Max decide to take a nap after all?"

She blew a breath out the side of her mouth but nodded. "I don't know how you did it, but you exhausted him."

"Don't you ever play pro wrestler with him?" Flipping over, he sat up. He must have studied her too long because she shifted and watched the next house over. "I can imagine you with a sequined cape and blond Goldilocks curls."

She laughed at that and seemed to relax. "And I thought I'd kept my alter ego a secret."

"Not from me."

It was a only a comeback in a silly conversation, but he was talking about something more than theatrical sporting events. From the way her eyes widened, Tricia must have recognized it, too. She probably thought she'd been keeping her loneliness a secret from everyone around her. But not from him.

She cleared her throat. "Are you feeling better today?"

"What?" Had he really forgotten about the accident the day before? He shouldn't be surprised. Whenever she was with him, his mind went blank, except for her in the center, and as scary as it was, there wasn't anything he could do to change that. "I'm all right, really."

Still, he didn't want her to continue talking about

the accident, so he changed the subject. "So what did you think of Christian Singles United?"

She studied him for several seconds, probably to see if he was really okay, before answering. "It was pretty nice. I think it will be a good ministry for our church. Do you think you'll go again?"

Only if you do. Instead of saying it, he shrugged. "Maybe. Depends on my schedule."

"Too many dates filling your calendar?"

The way she bit back a chuckle showed she'd surprised herself, as much as him, by saying that. Would it really matter to her if he saw other women? If it did, would that mean that she wanted him to *see* her?

"Just a lot of work."

She chewed her bottom lip. "You sure have gotten a good introduction to the people at Hickory Ridge this week. Are you going to keep attending?"

"I don't know. Would it be a problem for you?"

"Of course not." She said them too quickly for her words to ring true. "You know, you never said why you were searching for a new church home."

That third Coney dog he shouldn't have eaten started barking in his gut, but Brett steadied himself. If he wanted to get to know Tricia, to show her the kind of man he was, then he had to let her really know him, no matter how much it hurt to peel the scabs off old wounds.

He took a deep breath and began. "My old church just wasn't right anymore. I grew up in that church." He paused and then continued. "So did Claire."

"Your ex-fiancée."

So she'd remembered. He hadn't wanted to talk about it the night of the hockey game, and it didn't feel like a good idea now, either, but he was committed.

"We went on youth mission trips together. Helped conduct Backyard Bible Clubs in our neighborhoods. We had this crazy idea that we would operate some cool children's ministry together, you know…later." *After we were married.* He didn't say it, but her steady gaze as she sat cross-legged facing him told him she understood.

"The wedding was scheduled in that church."

"You'd already set a date?" She leaned in closer and tilted her head, showing she was listening. Interested.

"Date, invitations, tux, gown, cake—the whole she-bang. She called it off three weeks before the date." Blindsided him—that was the best way to describe it. "Said she didn't love me." He stared at the stripes on his cross-trainers for a few seconds. "And that was that."

"Well, that stinks."

He jerked his head up to see her sad smile, her empathetic gaze. At least he hadn't told her the humiliating truth that he and Claire had already named their future kids. Then Tricia might have cried on his behalf, and he would have been mortified. The tragedies in her life, were they pitted against his, would pummel his trivial excuses for problems into the ground. Her compassion for his scars only shamed him.

"Eh, water under the bridge."

"Where's Claire now?"

Brett shrugged and stared at the back of the house. The white paint was beginning to peel under the eaves. Somebody needed to take care of that. "Living the good life in Grosse Pointe, married to some investment banker."

"Her life can't be that good if she left you."

Tricia's softly spoken words drew his attention. "Thanks for saying that." She might have just been being nice, but it was so tempting to wish it meant more. And the way she chewed her lip and didn't meet his gaze made him wonder.

He changed the subject to relieve her discomfort... and his. "How long have you attended Hickory Ridge?"

"As long as I can remember. My parents were founding members." Her lips turned up, and her eyes took on a faraway look. "Most of the best memories from my childhood have been at the church."

Brett smiled back at her. "So we have something in common after all. We were always doing something at church, too. When we weren't there, the folks always had us in inner-city Detroit, working at a soup kitchen or charity thrift store."

"They sound like good people."

"They are. They always tried to be the best example of good Christians for their three kids." And they'd been successful with two out of three, but Brett wasn't in the mood to talk about Kyle. He wanted Tricia to know him, not his unsavory sibling.

"My parents were like that, too. They introduced me to Jesus when I was just a little girl."

He smiled at that, remembering his own profession of faith when he was still an optimistic twelve-year-old, having been forgiven his sins when he was too young to have collected a lengthy list. He didn't mention that, though, choosing to stick with the earlier subject. "Mom and Dad are one of those sick couples who seem like newlyweds after thirty-five years of marriage."

"Isn't that great?"

Brett answered with a shrug. He could have let the conversation die there; she wouldn't have noticed his omission. But for some reason, on this subject at least, he wanted to tell her more. All. "It's too bad they don't understand my choices."

Tricia watched him for several seconds until recognition appeared to dawn in her eyes. "They didn't want you to be a police officer?"

Brett lay back on the blanket and stared up at the gray sky, trying to decide how to explain something to her that he didn't understand himself. "It wasn't what they expected, I guess."

"But you can do so much good as a trooper. You get to make a difference."

He lifted up on his elbows and stared at her profile. The smirk he expected wasn't there. Then what was the explanation for the change in her feelings about his career? When she'd only seen the danger before, now she seemed to recognize a little of what he saw: the opportunity to help, the chance to make their community safer. Had she softened her stance on seeing him as well?

Tricia sensed Brett watching her, the skin on her cheek warming under his gaze. Sure, he had to be confused by what she'd said to him. She didn't know what to make of it herself. All she knew was that she wanted him to feel good about his work, and she resented his parents for not being proud of him. It hit a little too close to home.

She wished he would look away, wouldn't ask her silently to open up more than she was ready to, but he continued to observe her, waiting. Finally, she took a deep breath and dove in. "Parents should support their children, even if they don't agree with their decisions."

"You do support your children, no matter what. You're a wonderful mother."

Something warm blossomed inside Tricia's heart. Why it mattered so much that he thought her a good mother, she didn't bother to ponder. The reality was, it did. Even if she questioned his logic since he'd been present the other day when Rusty, Jr. had had his meltdown and she failed to deal with it effectively.

"That's not what I meant. My parents didn't want me to marry Rusty—thought we were too young. They never missed an opportunity to subtly remind him that he made me miss my chance to go to college.''

He was sitting up now, his arms crossed over his chest. "That's ridiculous. Why would they do that?" His indignation on her behalf warmed her more than his belief in her parenting skills.

"They're not bad. Really." How could she be so disloyal? They were her parents and deserved her respect. "After Rusty died, I don't know what I would have done without them. They moved back from their retirement home in Phoenix for six months to help out."

"But you've never quite forgiven them, have you?"

Brett's perceptive comment surprised her. She shook her head, but she didn't have a ready answer for him. Could he really read her so easily? If he could, she wondered what else he might know about her without her even telling him. She wasn't sure she wanted anyone to know her that well.

No one had known her like that since Rusty. But had her husband even had that kind of keen insight into her heart? If he had, he would have known how much his risk-taking worried her. He'd had to have known. So what would that have meant? That he didn't care enough about her worries to try to be more careful? Or maybe he'd just been unable to help himself.

She shook the thought away. She couldn't allow some strange notions to enter her mind and color her memories of her husband. Forcing her thoughts back to the simple question Brett had asked, she glanced at him. He had lowered himself back on the blanket and was pretending not to be watching her.

"I really need to forgive them, and maybe you could forgive your folks and Jenny, too."

He turned to face her but didn't lift his head off the blanket. "Jenny and I have already had it out. She feels bad for what she did and promised to keep my academy picture in her work locker from now on. She's even promised to try to help me get through to the folks."

"Well, that's good anyway."

"I don't know if my parents will ever understand, though. They had this plan for me and just can't envision me doing something else. Doing what I had to do."

"Do they say that police work is bad?"

He chuckled. "No, it's more subtle than that. It's the disappointed looks and the comments about how hard a time they're having keeping qualified staff at the dealership."

"You used to work there?"

"I was business manager. So, get this, Dad has hired and then pushed out three managers since I left. All of them were good guys. They just weren't quite… me."

"No pressure there." She said nothing for a few minutes and simply watched Brett, who looked so relaxed with his arms stretched out and his hands forming a pillow for his head. Unable to remember the last time she enjoyed respite like that, Tricia tried hard not to deny him his serenity. She held back a smile over the fleeting temptation to stretch out on the blanket next to him and look for cloud pictures in that same gray sky.

She chose to joke instead. ''Were you really all that amazing in your job that your dad can't replace you?''

He scrunched up his face in a dirty look. ''I did a good job, if that's what you're asking. But was I superior to those other guys? I doubt it. I was just Dad's big hope for someone to take over the family business.''

''Couldn't your sister or brother have done it?''

''Jenny studied nursing and made it clear from the start that she wasn't interested. And Kyle…well, Dad needed someone he could trust.''

''Why couldn't he trust him?''

His relaxed posture that had tempted her to jealousy tightened, his jaw took on a hard edge, and he crossed his arms over his chest. ''Let's just say that his most recent address came courtesy of the state penal system.''

Tricia's heart squeezed as she understood what it must have cost Brett to reveal that. A police officer's ultimate humiliation—a brother in prison. He faced her again, his gaze wary as if daring her to ask, too proud to beg her not to. Did he really think it would matter to her what his brother had done, that she was so fickle with her friendship that his news, though sad for him, would change anything?

Friends. They really had become that, hadn't they? Despite her reluctance to let anyone get close. And, strangely, she wasn't sorry. Brett was a good man, a man she was proud to know and privileged to call a friend.

"So you were the good son then?"

He raised an eyebrow but didn't answer.

"You know, the good son, the one who nearly kills himself trying to meet everyone's expectations, to never disappoint anyone."

Brett shook his head at first but stared up at the sky instead of looking at her. "Maybe once. But not anymore."

Tricia smiled at his profile. She had no doubt his need to please was still there, embedded in his personality, but the need hadn't stopped him from doing what he thought was right. At once, she was fiercely proud of the giant step he'd taken and the important work he did. "What changed?"

"It wasn't quite a two-by-four to the head, but close. When Claire dumped me, I found out that even jumping through all the hoops didn't guarantee a life like my parents have. I used to believe it did. I used to believe a lot of things." He turned his head toward the yelping beagle in the next fenced yard, perhaps to signal that the subject was closed.

Surprising and intense, emotion clogged Tricia's throat. *I used to believe a lot of things.* What else did he no longer believe? She'd sensed it from some of the things he'd said earlier, but now she was convinced. Brett might have gained the courage to follow his heart in at least one aspect of his life, but he had also lost something along the way. He seemed to only be going through the motions of his faith. He walked the Christian walk, even attended church and maybe still had a prayer life, but his life held no joy.

That just wasn't right. Sure, she knew she had no right to judge another person's heart, but she still found the situation unacceptable. Brett was such a good man, a kind man who was so intuitive he made her nervous. He probably even still considered himself a man of faith, but he deserved more than a life of empty ritual. Brett needed a chance to reclaim the joy of his walk with God.

When was the last time *she'd* experienced any joy? Tricia ignored the silly thought. Of course she remembered feeling joy—when Max mastered his two-wheeler early, when first Lani and then Rusty, Jr. learned to read, even on their memorable recent bowling outing. She'd even experienced it while attending a certain hockey game.

Of course, that wasn't the kind of joy she'd been thinking of, but she wasn't ready to answer that question when applying it to her faith. That didn't matter. Qualified to assist Brett or not, Tricia was determined to help him find his way.

The decision calmed her, as if a weight had been removed from her shoulders—one that made her wonder if being there with Brett was a mistake. It wasn't a mistake. He needed a friend, and she was only being there for him. That she happened to be having the best afternoon she'd had in a long time was only a great by-product.

Out of the corner of her eye, she watched him for several seconds, still seemingly determined not to look back at her. Tricia took a deep breath for courage and lay back on the blanket, keeping a careful distance between them, then stared up at the sky. Sunshine batted against a solid wall of clouds, making the gray scene deeper blue in some places, but the rays couldn't seem to break through. Still, the warmth the sun couldn't provide spread through her insides at just the idea of feeling so small in the scheme of God's creation. Small but not forgotten.

"It feels great, doesn't it?" Brett asked, interrupting her thoughts. Already he'd settled back on the blanket, resting his head in the cradle of his hands. "Just being here. Just being."

"Doesn't it make you feel small, staring at the sky?"

"No, it reminds me of the stars," he said. "I remember this verse in Psalms that says, God 'determines the number of the stars, He gives to all of them their names.'"

His words felt like a deep breath, expanding in her lungs, filling her need for air, for life. She chuckled as much to relieve the anxiety the thought produced as to remark at the irony of the Scripture he'd quoted. Without looking, she sensed him watching her, his eyebrows probably drawn together quizzically.

''That's strange. We're both looking up at God's same sky, and you're thinking stars, while I'm thinking lilies. I remember memorizing Luke 12:27 as a little girl. 'Consider the lilies, how they grow; they neither toil nor spin; yet I tell you, even Solomon in all his glory was not arrayed like one of these.'''

Sitting up, he turned to look at her. ''It's impossible to look at creation without thinking about God's word.''

Tricia sat up, too, unable to resist smiling. He seemed to want to find his way back to God as much as she wanted to help him find it.

She didn't know how long they'd sat facing each other, touching only with their gazes, and perhaps a like-minded spirit, when a crash broke the trance.

At the gate, Lani and Rusty, Jr. stood, their backpacks slung over their shoulders, the jackets they should have been wearing likely tucked in with the books. The gate one of them had slammed still hung open against the house's siding.

Tricia shot back from Brett and came to her feet, her throat dry, her heart pounding.

''Mommy, where were you?'' Lani asked as she zipped across the yard. ''You weren't waiting out front when we got off the bus.''

Lani dropped her book bag on the blanket and plopped down next to Brett. He sat just where he had before, appearing calm. Not the way she must have looked. As if she'd been caught doing something wrong.

At least one of them didn't feel guilty.

Lani was already busy chattering with Brett, so Tricia turned her attention to her second child. Rusty, Jr. stood like a statue, his backpack still dangling from his shoulders. He clenched tiny fists at his sides, his fury visible in his tight jaw.

Tricia hurried toward him, not sure what to expect or what to say. But the boy only slipped past her, headed for his obvious target. Brett.

"Why don't you go away?" he shrieked.

Brett came to his feet, his hands going wide in a pose he'd probably used dozens of times to calm tense situations. The six-year-old, though, wouldn't stop. The child pummeled the man's stomach with ineffectual strikes, but Brett didn't even try to contain his hands.

"Rusty, Jr., you stop it this instant," Tricia shouted, but her son couldn't seem to hear her. Or he wasn't listening.

Lani had jumped up and now looked confused, jerking her head back and forth to watch Brett and her brother. "Quit it, Rusty, Jr. Why are you hitting Mr. Brett?"

Finally, Brett grasped both of the boy's hands in one of his and sidestepped a kick aimed his way. "Okay, buddy, are you done now? You need to get control."

But even when his hands were stilled, the child kept whipping his head back and forth. "You're not our daddy!'' he wailed. ''We don't need a new daddy! Go away! We don't want you!''

Brett brushed his free hand through the boy's hair, his touch surprisingly gentle considering that Rusty, Jr. still raged against him. ''It's okay, kiddo. I don't want to be your dad. But I'd like to be your friend.''

''I don't want you to be my friend. I don't like you.''

To his credit, Brett only chuckled. ''Oh, that's too bad because I like you a lot, you and Max and Lani.''

As much as what he'd said, Tricia appreciated what he hadn't mentioned. That he obviously liked their mother a lot, too, to be putting up with this abuse. But an announcement like that probably would have added to the boy's rage.

''Well, I don't like you.''

''Rusty Evan Williams, Jr., I want you to apologize this very instant.''

But Brett only shook his head at her, as if to tell her not to say anything else, before lowering his gaze to the boy again. ''Fair enough.''

No one spoke for a few minutes. That was when Tricia became aware of the sobbing. She glanced over at Lani, who cried silent tears beside her friend and her troubled younger brother. But hers wasn't the sound Tricia had heard. Through the storm door, little Max stood there, awake from his nap and shaking all over.

At once Tricia's heart shattered. The child who had been too young to understand his father's death two years before, whose only tears had been when he'd watched his mother, brother and sister crying, bawled now over another situation he couldn't possibly understand. The brother he loved had attacked his friend. He wouldn't see how Rusty, Jr. had felt threatened by the newcomer—how his brother would worry that they'd forget his father altogether—only that the boy had struck a grown-up.

Her heart pounding, Tricia raced toward the door, opened it and clasped her youngest child to her middle.

"Mommy…Mr. Brett…Rusty, Jr.," Max said, speaking the names between gasps.

"It's all right, sweetheart."

She watched as Brett finally released his hold on Rusty, Jr. The six-year-old only looked at him with a confused expression, as if he wasn't quite certain what had just happened between them, and then the child turned and rushed past her into the house. Lani stood beside Brett, a shocked expression on her face. Tricia held out an arm, and her daughter moved to fill the space next to her.

Tricia took a deep breath and met Brett's troubled gaze. "It might be best if you go now."

But he shook his head. "I want to help. I'll stay if you want me to."

"No, we're okay. Everything's going to be fine."

Brett nodded and, with a wave and a smile for the children, turned and walked out the backyard gate.

Only it wasn't fine. The way her older son had acted out was only a symptom of wounds that hadn't healed, no matter how she'd told herself otherwise. No, it wasn't fine. And it wouldn't be anytime soon.

Chapter Ten

That night as she put away the last few dishes and picked up the last of the fashion doll clothes and action figures, Tricia couldn't remember being so exhausted since the early days following her husband's death. The children had been so quiet all night that the usually calming silence of their sleeping hours only agitated her.

As she'd kissed the children good-night, Lani, always so grown up, had squeezed her mother's arm to show support, forcing her to fight back a sob.

"Mommy, Mr. Brett won't be coming to our house anymore, will he?" Lani had given voice to the question that had flitted on the edges of Tricia's consciousness most of the night.

"I don't know, honey." She didn't know. Nor could she acknowledge the plea inside her, not when those selfish needs for companionship were unwelcome at a time when her focus needed to be on her children.

All night Max had been clingy and out of sorts, but Rusty, Jr. had been the hardest to put to bed. If only he'd been belligerent the way she'd expected him to be, the situation would have been bearable. But the docile, quiet child she'd tucked beneath his blankets hadn't seemed like her son at all.

Already this afternoon she'd called the grief counselor's office and set up additional sessions for Rusty, Jr. and for the rest of them. It was high time she admitted that they weren't okay the way she'd been trying so hard to convince everyone they were.

She was so tired. Her arms hung heavy, and her neck ached with the effort of holding her head upright. Exhausted or not, she wouldn't be able to sleep tonight, not when her children were so stricken.

Rubbing against the strain at her temples, she headed down the short hall to her bedroom, stopping first at Lani's room. She dropped a quick kiss on the sleeping child's brow and then crossed to the boys' room.

At first, she thought her weary eyes were playing tricks on her. From the streetlight stealing into the room, she could see that one of the twin beds—the one Rusty, Jr. slept in—was empty. Her throat constricted, but Tricia shook her head, forcing herself not to go into one of her classic mom overreactions. There had to be an explanation for Rusty, Jr. being out of bed.

She glanced over at Max's bed, a reasonable first guess since the boys often bunked together instead of sleeping in their own beds. But Max was alone, nestled in his pile of covers, his face pressed into the pillow.

Tricia's hands became damp, and her heart raced. She couldn't panic. She needed to think. Hitting the wall switch to send light flooding into the room, she knelt between the twin beds and looked under both of them. Nothing.

Only when she leaned back on her haunches did she notice the gaping hole of a clue she'd missed before. The window, open to provide a cool evening breeze and a bit of light to ease the boys' nighttime fears, was missing a screen. Tricia gasped and threw a hand over her mouth. Max startled in his sleep and cried out but didn't awaken.

No longer able to contain her panic, she jerked her head back and forth, trying to find an explanation when there was none. The closet door was open, so he couldn't have hidden there. The dresser was pushed against the wall. The bathroom was down the hall, so Rusty, Jr. would have passed her to reach it. Where was he? Why couldn't he just pop out and yell "boo" so this horrible practical joke could end? Finally, her gaze landed on her son's pillow. Usually, "Sad Dog," her son's precious beanbag beagle named for its woeful eyes, would have been there waiting for the boy's return. But it, like Rusty, Jr., was gone. Clearer than a note would have been, the toy's absence signaled that her son didn't plan on coming back.

Tricia raced to the kitchen and grabbed the phone, dialing a number that was automatic to her. "Reverend Bob, this is Tricia." She drew a breath into her burning lungs. "Rusty, Jr. is missing. I think he's run away."

"Keep breathing slowly, Tricia. Everything's going to be all right," the minister said in his comforting voice. "Have you called the police yet?"

"Not...yet." She tried to inhale again, her lungs refusing to accept the new influx of oxygen. "I just found out he's not...here."

"You call 9-1-1, and I'll do the rest. I'll call some of the church members. Then I'll bring Hannah with me so she can watch Lani and Max."

As a fog settled over her mind, refusing to let her focus, Tricia hung up the phone and dialed the Milford Police Department. As soon as the dispatcher promised to send an officer, she lowered the receiver.

Then on an impulse, she picked it up again. If her mind wasn't clear about her plan, her fingers seemed to know just what they were doing as they dialed.

Brett's tired voice answered on the second ring. "Lancaster."

"Brett, it's Tricia." She paced from the boys' bedroom to the living room and back.

"Tricia, what is it? Where are you?"

"I'm here at home, but Rusty, Jr. is missing."

A clanging noise came through the line as he must have dropped the phone. It startled her out of her daze.

"Sorry about that." All sleepiness had vanished

from his voice. He'd become the practiced police officer, searching for clues. "Do you believe he's been abducted?" But he didn't give her a chance to answer. "Tricia, I want you to get Max and Lani together and get out of that house. The suspect might still be—"

She stopped pacing, her thoughts clearing. He'd jumped to the same conclusion she had briefly, but she sensed inside they'd both been mistaken. "Brett, no."

"You need to get out. I want you safe. You shouldn't be—" But finally he stopped himself, perhaps realizing that he sounded less like a police officer and more like someone who cared too much about her.

"Listen. Rusty, Jr. is out there somewhere, but I don't think someone took him. I was awake, and I didn't hear anything. The room isn't even messed up…beyond the usual. You know he would have fought. And he took Sad Dog with him, the dog that he always keeps in his bed."

While she'd been so busy trying to convince Brett, Tricia suddenly felt less certain. *Please, God, let me be right. And let Rusty, Jr. be okay.*

"Are you going to be all right?" he asked finally.

"I'm fine. Reverend Bob and some of the others should be here any minute."

"And the local police?"

"They should be here soon."

He made a muffled sound into the phone, as if he were pulling a shirt over his head, before speaking into the receiver again. "I'm on my way."

Tricia heard him click off the phone, but still she

held it to her ear for several seconds, a sense of calm filtering through the fog of her fear. She'd asked God to keep Rusty, Jr. safe, and she was confident her son was in good hands. His hands. Had God also sent Brett to support her and help her to believe? She wasn't sure. She just felt safer knowing Brett would be there, too.

Brett had to force himself not to press the accelerator to the floor on the trip from Brighton back to Milford. But he didn't want to risk losing more time by mistakenly getting pulled over by another police officer. Not for the first time, he wished the state police had a take-home program for patrol cars, but that wasn't important now. The only thing that mattered was getting to Tricia and helping her find her son.

He'd asked her about an abduction, but he, too, considered it unlikely. It would have been too coincidental for Rusty, Jr. to have been abducted on the same day he'd made such a spectacle of himself about not needing anyone. No, Brett's gut feeling, which he'd learned to trust implicitly, told him the boy had run away. All that yelling had only been a mask for the pain of a tortured little boy.

Brett's instinct was to help anyone who needed it, but was he man enough for this job? The boy's scars were deep, his problems bigger than a do-gooder cop could expect to handle. Did a child ever heal completely after losing a parent? More than that, Brett wondered if the boy's accusation had been right on.

Was he really trying to step into Rusty Williams's shoes, filling that man's place in Tricia and her children's hearts?

If he was, then he had no right. That and no sense. Tricia would never let go of the memories of her husband in order to make a place for him in her heart. Rusty, Jr. had already told Brett what he thought about him.

He was being ridiculous thinking of all that, when a first-grader was somewhere out in the dark—lonely and scared. Tricia hadn't called him because she wanted him to take care of her family, either. She'd called him for no other reason than because he was a police officer. Too bad he was too tense to find humor in the irony of that. When she did need help from law enforcement, it never hurt to have a friend who just happened to wear a uniform.

In half the time it would have taken him if he'd followed posted speed limits, Brett arrived in front of Tricia's house, resentful of the drivers of all those cars already parked there, including the village police patrol car. What had he expected? To arrive first and to reach her when she needed him most? To save the day? Okay, he had, but he was over his illusions now. He just wanted to help. He wanted to make it all right for Tricia's family.

Brett hurried up the walk, already seeing several church members inside the glass storm door. Reverend Bob motioned him inside when he reached the porch.

He gripped the minister's forearm as soon as he came inside. "What do we know so far?"

Reverend Bob lowered his gaze to his arm until Brett released him, but then he smiled. "We've just been praying. The situation is in God's hands."

"So you're just going to sit here and wait for God to perform His will?"

The minister's head jerked back, and his eyes widened, two reminders that Brett wasn't handling the situation with the same practiced calm he used in investigating auto accidents, larcenies and battery cases. He had to get control of his emotions.

"Of course not, man," the youth minister Andrew Westin said as he stepped over and gripped Brett's shoulder. "We were just praying before we went out searching for Rusty, Jr." He indicated with his head toward the kitchen where beyond the half wall Tricia sat with a uniformed Milford police officer. "Tricia's helping with the police report."

Brett blew out a frustrated breath. "Sorry about that." He paused and glanced at Reverend Bob to include him in his apology. "Where will the search begin?"

"Do you want me to introduce you to the other police officer?" Andrew said, already walking in that direction.

Brett raised a hand to stop him. "Maybe later. They're busy." Anyway, he didn't want to be there as Trooper Lancaster. He was there as Tricia's friend.

What are you guys waiting for? he wanted to shout

at the crowd in the living room. Instead he slipped down the hall to peek, guessing which room would belong to the boys. At the end of the hall he cracked open the door on the right. From the familiar rose-petal scent drifting into his senses, he recognized Tricia's room, even before he took in the mauve decor with its many feminine touches. Quickly, he backed out of the room and turned to the one across the hall from it.

This time, the hallway light skimmed across two twin beds, one of them empty. Tricia was right. The room showed no obvious struggle, just some of the regular messiness of rambunctious boys. Rusty, Jr.'s bed looked as if he'd just tossed back the blankets and bailed out.

Brett's gaze drifted to Max's bed where the child still snuggled under the covers, oblivious to the story unfolding around him. How the child could have slept through so much activity, he couldn't imagine.

He switched off the hall light and moved about the room in silence, using a miniature flashlight to look for clues in a case that wasn't his. A case that meant more to him than any other had in months.

Where would you go, Rusty, Jr.? What message did you leave behind? Okay, he already knew the boy had taken his favorite toy. So he wanted to take his special things with him. Brett flashed his light on the bulletin board where snapshots plastered every inch of the cork material—except two square-shaped holes. He didn't have to quiz Tricia to know that the missing pictures would be of the father the little boy thought he couldn't live without.

He steadied his flashlight on the other pictures. Rusty, Jr.'s soccer team. Max's preschool class. But most were of all or part of the Williams family, playing together, laughing together. Did he really think he could ever be a part of that? He'd never be able to compete with the man pictured holding a newborn baby or proudly holding up a fishing pole with a puny-looking fish hanging from the line.

Maybe he could never be that man they all obviously missed, but there was one thing he could do. He could bring Tricia's son back to her.

As he was backing out of the room and closing the door, something touched his back, startling him. Lani stood behind him, looking tinier than usual in a long ruffled nightgown with only her toes peeking out the bottom. She rubbed her sleepy eyes and looked up at him.

"What's going on, Mr. Brett?" She glanced down the hall at the other adults, too busy planning their strategy to notice the child in the darkened hallway.

"Everything's fine, sweetheart. Now try to get some sleep, okay?"

She just stood there. "Reverend Bob said it's a sin to lie."

Despite the tension surrounding him, Brett smiled at the intuitive seven-year-old. He lifted her into his arms and brushed a hand through her short, dark hair. The child felt light in his arms, still so young and yet so old. Still three years away from middle school, she'd already lived through more pain than any child should ever have to endure. He wasn't about to let this little girl or her youngest brother or her mother face another tragedy.

"And Reverend Bob's right. Okay, I won't lie to you. Things aren't so good right now, but they are going to be fine. I promise."

Promising was a mistake. He shouldn't—couldn't—when he had no better idea than anyone else where Rusty, Jr. would have gone. Or what might have happened to him *after* he'd left this house of his own free will.

"It's Rusty, Jr., isn't it? He's gone, isn't he?"

Brett took a deep breath, wondering how much he should tell. It was Tricia's place—not his—to let her family know what had happened, no matter how much he wanted to protect the mother from having to tell and the children from having to hear. "Well...you see," he started out awkwardly, pausing for some inspiration.

"Is it true, Mommy?" Lana asked as someone flipped the hall switch, sending yellow light to create a melding of light and shadow in the narrow hallway.

Brett turned to face Tricia, who had approached behind him where only Lani could see. He lowered the child to the ground and rested a hand on her shoulder as she turned to her mother.

"Yes, honey, Rusty, Jr. is missing, but we're trying to find him. That's why all of these people are here...

to help.'' At her last words, Tricia's gaze connected with Brett's, her thanks evident in her stark expression.

Help? He hadn't done a single thing for her besides hightailing it from his house to hers at ten-thirty at night. Her gratitude shamed him. Unable to prevent himself, he clasped Tricia's hand and squeezed it, trying to let her know that, although he hadn't been much help so far, he was about to change that.

Tricia nodded at him and, slipping out of his grasp, led her daughter to the crowd of adults in the living room. Hannah, who had left her own child with her baby-sitter, came forward and wrapped the girl in her arms.

''Okay, the Milford officer just left, so here's where we are,'' Tricia told the crowd. ''Village police will be patrolling some of the areas, but we need to go out, too.''

Amid the chatter that followed, Brett held up his hands for silence. ''We'll cover more ground if we divide up. Reverend Bob, can you cover the school grounds?'' He didn't wait for the minister's nod before he turned to the couple beside him. ''Rick and Charity, I'd like you to cover both sides of Main Street between the new shopping plaza and the train trestle. Check along the storefronts, but also check out the rear parking areas.''

''Will do,'' Rick answered with a nod.

At least no one had said anything about Brett taking

charge of the situation. He'd had to do something, and at least this was one thing he had under his control.

"Okay, Andrew and Serena, you take Central Park and the River Bend Playscape area. Make sure you check down by the river behind the trees."

A few of the adults standing near him shifted, as though they, too, were worrying about the many monsters of the night that could threaten a boy who wasn't even kidnapped. His own adrenaline flow was producing dozens of scenarios—none of them good.

"Julia, I'd like you to take the Kroger plaza." Then he turned to Tricia. "I want you to stay here by the phone. Everyone will check in with you by cell phone. Also, then you'll be the first to know when anyone—us or the police—locates him."

Hannah stepped forward, still holding Lani's hand. "What about me?"

"Can you handle all the kids?" Brett glanced around the room, for the first time noticing that though several church families were represented, their children weren't.

"Mary Nelson has Rebecca, Tessa and Seth at her house," Hannah explained. "We'll be fine here." She led Lani into the kitchen for a promised late-night snack.

"Good, then Tricia will be able to leave here as soon as we find…anything." He didn't take time to spell out any of the possible scenarios that awaited them as they hunted for the first-grader. He didn't have to.

As the rest of the church members put on their jackets and stepped onto the porch, Tricia moved closer to Brett.

"Where will you be going?"

"I'm going to cover the walking area and check out a few hunches." He opened the door and then patted his pocket. "I'll keep in touch by my phone."

When he would have expected her to wave, she rested a hand on his forearm. "Thanks so much for coming. I really appreciate your…being here." At first, she took a deep breath, as if it could plaster over the deteriorating walls of her composure, but then she just let them crumble.

Brett's arms closed around her as her knees seemed to buckle. The others were already in their cars, pulling away from the curb, so he stepped back inside and let the door fall closed. For several seconds, he only held her, willing his strength into her at a time when she needed it. At the same time, he tried to absorb her fear and anguish along with her strangled cries. When she stiffened, he knew she'd reclaimed the courage he'd witnessed in her so many times before.

He released his hold on her, and she stepped back. The words were out of his mouth before he could stop them. "I promise I won't let anything happen to him, Tricia."

She rolled her lips inward and squeezed her eyes shut for several seconds, but finally met his gaze and nodded. Again, he was making promises he had no right to make in a situation over which he had no control. What made him want to give anything—his life even—to make Tricia's world right for her? He couldn't think about that, couldn't think about anything at all, except locating Rusty, Jr. He'd promised the boy's mother he would. Now he prayed that God would help him keep his promise.

Chapter Eleven

Two hours later, Brett's eyes burned, and that last cup of coffee seemed to stomp on his nerves rather than supply a much-needed dose of caffeine to his brain. But still he drove. There had to be something he was forgetting.

Everyone had already checked in with Tricia. No sign of Rusty, Jr. at any of their assigned areas. *Where are you?* he asked into the darkness, as if God would just suddenly place the boy in plain sight beside the next streetlight.

Lord, there's something I'm missing here, something I'm forgetting. Please open my mind to all the possibilities. His prayer added another verse to the litany he'd spoken inside since climbing behind the wheel.

Again, he turned on Atlantic Avenue, the opposite way this time, hoping that the change in direction would give him new theories. But it was an old theory that kept needling at him. Finally, he gave up and dialed Tricia's number.

"Any word?" he asked as soon as she answered.

"Nothing. I hoped you'd be calling with some."

If wishing were news, he'd have a lot to tell her. "Sorry. But I do have some questions about your husband."

There was silence on the line for a few seconds before she answered. "Okay. But why now?"

"Just a hunch. Did you see the bulletin board in the boys' room? There were some pictures that looked like they'd been removed."

She didn't answer, but from the jostling, he guessed she was walking down the hall to the room. A small squeak suggested she'd opened the door.

"I guessed they were of Rusty, Jr. and his dad."

More shuffling and then silence. "They were."

"Tricia, it's not surprising that he would have taken pictures of his dad with him if he planned to run away."

"I was in one of them—just the three of us."

"Of you, too. Sure, he'd want pictures of the people he loved most."

The anguish he'd heard in her voice earlier had returned when she spoke again. "What do you want to know?"

"Tell me some of the activities your husband did with Rusty, Jr." He just couldn't bring himself to call the man by name, even when his presence was so much a part of everything happening that night.

"We all went to church together. Rusty liked to splash with the kids in that oversize kiddy pool. He would take them ice skating on the rink at Central Park."

Brett shook his head in the darkness. Obviously, he was barking up the proverbial wrong tree and wasting her time when maybe someone was trying to call in with important news. But he prompted her anyway. "Anything else you can think of?"

"He always watched the Lions games with them. Said when they were older he'd take them to one." Her voice grew wistful as she spoke the last.

"No. Other things. Small things. Did they play baseball or go bowling or play golf?"

"Remember, Rusty, Jr. was just four years old when his dad died." She took an audible breath. "He was a little young for some of that."

"I see what you mean—"

"I always said he was too young for fishing, too, but Rusty took him anyway, though I don't think he ever had a hook on his pole."

Fishing? Ideas swirled through his mind again where they'd become scarce before. But no matter what he thought, he couldn't tell Tricia, couldn't raise her hopes. In case he was wrong. "Okay, thanks. I'm going to look a while longer."

"Are you sure? You don't have to—"

"I'll get back to you if I find anything," he said before clicking off the phone.

Already, he was heading back to Main Street and the points where the Huron River passed through downtown Milford. It took him a few stops at various fishing spots, but just beyond the bridge across from the park, he spotted a small figure with a fishing pole.

He whispered a prayer of thanksgiving as he parked the car and made his way down the riverbank to the area lit by streetlights. "Hey, pal."

Instead of running as Brett expected he would, Rusty, Jr. only snuggled deeper into the jacket that covered his light pajamas and said nothing. Untied sneakers without socks covered the boy's feet. Sitting on the cold, damp ground, the boy had to be freezing, but he would never admit it.

"A lot of people have been looking for you."

The boy shrugged, but his shoulders sagged even farther forward. He swung his simple bamboo fishing pole over the water. It had no hook.

Somehow Brett managed not to smile as he took a seat on the ground next to him. This was too important to the mother and to the child for him to make light of it. "I bet you used to fish right here with your dad."

The boy jerked his head and looked up at him for several seconds before giving an almost imperceptible nod. "I never caught no fish."

Brett made a show of studying the water instead of the boy. "Fishing's hard sometimes."

"I need a hook."

Brett nodded. "That will make it work better."

"Daddy never let me use a hook."

His heart squeezed with anguish for the boy's past, but what of his future? Could he help him see a brighter one? "You were pretty young then."

"I'm big now." Those little shoulders straightened with a male bravado he was only beginning to learn.

"You're right. I bet you're old enough to use an actual rod and reel now, with a hook and everything."

Why was it that this look at the future and not memories from the past sent tears streaming down the child's cheeks? Brett longed to grab the boy and hug him, but he wasn't sure whether Rusty, Jr. was ready to accept his comfort. So he sat and, grabbing a few rocks in the grass, skipped them across the river.

Rusty, Jr. shoved the backs of his hands over his eyes. "Mommy isn't a good fisher."

Brett couldn't help studying the boy's profile then. Was he asking what he thought he was asking? "I like to go fishing."

"Are you any good?"

"Pretty good, I guess. I know how to bait hooks, too." He paused for several seconds before he took a chance. "I could teach you…if you want to sometime."

Rusty, Jr. lifted a shoulder and dropped it. "Sometime, maybe."

"I don't have a good fishing partner. Do you think we could go fishing together?"

Instead of another shrug, as Brett had expected, the boy nodded. "If Mommy says it's okay."

"Speaking of your mom, she's really worried about you. Don't you think we should call her?"

"Is she real mad?"

Brett shook his head and lifted himself up off the ground. "No, I think she's more worried. You could have really gotten hurt, running away at night."

"I'm okay."

"I know you are, but how about we go back to your house anyway? I'm tired, so I need to get home to bed." Brett fumbled in his shirt pocket for his cell phone. "Here, you can call your mom on our way."

Brett took a few steps, hoping Rusty, Jr. would follow, and released a held breath when he did.

"You sure she won't be mad?"

"I'm sure she'll be glad to see you." Brett couldn't wait to get the boy home. Not because he'd be able to keep his promise to Tricia, either. He only wanted to see the relief in her eyes when she saw that her son was okay. He wanted to see her eyes light with happiness and her lips form a smile when she realized everything was going to be all right.

"Mommy, is Mr. Brett your boyfriend?" Rusty, Jr. asked as Tricia pulled up the covers in his bed an hour later.

Tricia's breath caught in her throat, and she peeked behind her to see if anyone was standing in the doorway to the boys' bedroom and could have overheard.

No one was there. She released her breath in slow stream. "No, honey. He's my friend—your friend, too." After tonight, with all he'd done for her family, for her son in particular, she couldn't imagine calling him anything else. "We only went on one date a while ago, remember?"

His silence hinted he'd accepted the answer, so she tucked the sheet under his arms. But then he spoke again. "Will you go on more dates with him?"

Tricia shot a glance again at the empty space in the hallway before she met her child's sleepy gaze. "Why, sweetheart? Would you like it if I did?" She didn't have to wait long for his nod.

"Mr. Brett said he would take me fishing."

She smiled in the darkness. "I'm sure he will, honey." She was beginning to be sure of a lot of things about Brett Lancaster, most of all that he was a good and honorable man and one whose company she enjoyed far more than any widow should.

Several minutes passed, but Tricia stayed until her son fell asleep, more for her comfort than his. Even after the boy was sleeping peacefully, she watched to see his chest rise and fall in a slow cadence.

He was alive. He was safe. She could finally breathe, knowing both of those things. Earlier tonight, she'd wondered if she would ever breathe again if, after all of this searching, they'd discovered the worst. The "what ifs" had nearly eaten her alive. What if her assumption had been wrong and Rusty, Jr. had been abducted, her denial allowing their trail to go cold? What if her son really had run away but had been unfortunate enough to be hit by a car or to drown in the Huron River or a hundred other equally awful outcomes?

It was over. None of those things had happened, and yet now she couldn't stop shaking, tragic images in her mind suddenly more vivid in the aftermath than during the crisis. Rusty, Jr. looked so small as he slept, not much bigger than Max, who had somehow slept through the whole event. Her sweet boy, barely old enough to catch a pop fly, and yet she'd nearly lost him today.

Dear God, thank You for Your loving hands that protected my child tonight. And thank You for sending Brett to bring Rusty, Jr. back to me. Amen.

Brett. Her heart squeezed at just the memory of him bounding through the door, her son in his soggy superhero pajamas getting a free ride on his back. Rusty, Jr. had already called her from Brett's cell phone, and she'd known they were coming home, but somehow it had still been a shock to see the two of them together. Laughing together.

She needed to get back out to the living room to Brett and all her other friends who'd come to help. Touching Rusty, Jr.'s hand to prove to herself again that he was safe, she stood and slipped out into the hall. A roomful of friends, all offering concern and compassion, awaited her in the living room, but she desperately needed some time to be alone, to curl up in a ball and recover.

When she reached the living room, she was just that. Alone. Maybe she wasn't as ready to be by herself as she'd thought. The room felt too small, the air too thick.

"How's he doing?"

She startled at the sound of Brett's low voice. Funny, though, just knowing he was there comforted her. She could breathe again, so she took several slow breaths before she spoke.

"I thought everyone had left."

"Everyone but me."

The teakettle behind him started to whistle, so he lifted it off the burner. That was when she noticed the two ceramic mugs, tea bags already waiting inside them.

"Thanks for staying."

Brett lifted the mugs off the counter and settled them on the table, taking a seat in front of one. "It's late. I have my second day off tomorrow, so I told everyone to go home to their families, and I would wait to make sure you were okay."

"That was nice of you." She sat at the table and wrapped her hands around the mug, its warmth such a contrast to the ice that had curled around her bones while she'd waited for word on her son.

"Hey, I'm just that kind of guy."

He'd meant it as a joke, and she knew it, but she still answered, "Yes, you are." Because he was.

He met her gaze for a few seconds and then lowered his to concentrate on his drink, squeezing the tea bag out by wrapping it around a spoon. "You didn't tell me how Rusty, Jr. is doing."

"He's sleeping. Like nothing ever happened."

"But something did happen, didn't it?"

Tricia's breath caught in her throat, and she gripped the mug tighter. He'd given voice to the very thought circling in her mind. How could she answer his question? That her life had nearly ended that night?

"Did I thank you before for finding him?"

He tilted his head and studied her. "At least a dozen times since we got back."

"Thanks for offering to take him fishing. He's excited about that."

"It will be fun."

The room became silent as Brett paused to sip his tea. Tricia scrambled to fill the empty space.

"I took the kids fishing recently, but I guess my angling skills aren't up to par."

Again, there was a long pause as Brett watched her, his eyes too sweet, too compassionate, when she needed to regain her equilibrium in her spinning world.

"Tricia, is this how we're going to do this? Are we going to pretend nothing happened and that I had a good ol' time inviting Rusty, Jr. to go fishing?"

She shook her head, as much to push his suggestion away as to clear her thoughts. "Do we really need to hash it out?"

"No, but is it better to gloss over it like it didn't happen?"

She raised a hand, tried to discourage him from pressing forward when that positive movement could only have negative effect. Yes, she wanted to pretend it had never happened. If only pretending could make it so. But she doubted she'd ever wake up again without that cold sweat of wondering what if it had turned out differently.

His hand suddenly closed over the one she'd been extending to dissuade him, its grip reassuring but firm. "You spent most of tonight thinking you'd lost your son, and now you don't want to talk about it?"

She yanked her hand away. "No, I don't—"

"You thought you'd lost Rusty, Jr. forever. It was just like losing his father all over again, wasn't it?"

Tricia jerked back from the table so quickly that her dinette chair crashed to the floor. She didn't care. Her heart pounded. Her eyes burned, but she refused to cry. Couldn't cry.

"You have no right to talk about it." She backed away from him and out of the kitchen, as if he was chasing her with his concern. "You don't know— You don't have any idea what any of it was like— then or now."

"So tell me what it was like." He lifted up from the chair but stood where he was, tucking his thumbs through his belt loops. "I want to know. I want to understand."

Tricia squeezed her eyes shut and shook her head. "That's just it. Nobody understands."

When she opened her eyes again, colorful dots of

light danced on the wall, refusing to let her see clearly. "Everyone wants me to just get over it. To move on. To forget. But I can't forget."

Tricia wasn't talking about the night's events, and Brett knew it. She was talking about the man he'd never known, the memory he could never compete with, but still his heart ached with the need to comfort her. He longed to bound over the chair, still laying on its back in the floor, so he could pull her into his arms. But her rigid posture—her arms straight, her hands fisted—telegraphed that she wasn't ready to accept his empathy.

She was right, he didn't have any clue what she'd gone through two years before, let alone tonight. But he did know what it was like to care about someone, to hurt for her hurts and to feel helpless with the need to protect her. Gripping the back of his chair as he stood, he fought to maintain his careful distance from her, just as she battled back the tears that shone in her eyes.

Neither spoke for what had to have been a few minutes, until finally Brett shattered the silence, speaking as softly as he could. "I don't want you to forget."

She jerked her eyes to meet his gaze and then shook her head hard. "Then what do you want from me?"

The pleading in her voice was his undoing, and Brett started toward her, maneuvering around the chair rather than righting it. He ignored the voice inside that suggested he might need the connection more than she did.

Tricia halted him by holding both hands up in front of her, her fingers spread wide. "You wanted to know if tonight was like then. Yes. Are you happy now? Are you satisfied now that you know I sat here all night waiting for my world to end?"

Still too many steps away from her to grip her hands, Brett shook his head. "No, Tricia—"

"Then what? What is it you want to know? That part of me was already dead? That it died with Rusty when he fell off that building?"

Her words sliced at his skin as he took two steps closer to her. Why had he asked when he couldn't bear to hear her answers, to know that she could never care about him the way she had her husband?

"Let it go, Tricia." He heard himself saying those words when he really wanted to say, *Let me in.*

She backed away two steps and crossed her arms. "No, I don't want to let it go. I can't." A long, jagged breath fell heavy from her lungs. "Then there'll be nothing left."

"You still have so much. You've got God, your kids, your friends, your church."

Tricia only shook her head, tears escaping from the corners of her eyes. "My baby. I could have lost…my baby…tonight."

By the time the single sob escaped her, he'd already pulled her into his arms, his embrace fierce. "But he's fine, Tricia. He's fine. Yes, he needs more time with a grief counselor—you do, too—but he's going to be okay."

She no longer even tried to stop the tears that rolled down her face to her chin. "He was out there...all alone. Look what could have...happened."

"It didn't." He brushed a hand through her soft, dark hair, comforting her as he would have a child. "God was there for him the whole time."

Tricia rested her hands on Brett's biceps and stepped back from his embrace. "But I wasn't. Don't you see? Rusty, Jr. needed me, and I couldn't see his needs. I couldn't protect my own child."

Tricia's conversation drifted from tangent to tangent, but they were all loosely sewn together by a single thread that said she'd failed—to love enough, know enough, do enough—to prevent her family from experiencing pain.

His arms ached to hold her again, but he stayed where he was, facing her. Though mere inches separated them, they seemed to be miles apart.

"Listen to me, Tricia. You're a good mother. I've never seen anyone who loved her kids the way you love yours. They know you love them."

"But I couldn't protect him." With the back of her hands, she brushed at the tears on her cheeks. Already, there seemed to be fewer of them to wipe away.

"No parent can. Not completely. But he's going to be okay. He's in his bed right now. Safe."

"Because of you."

Their gazes met then, and the pride so visible in her eyes unnerved him. Did she think he was a hero? That couldn't have been further from the truth. If he were a hero, he would have helped her without the ulterior motive of getting closer to her. He brushed away her praise with a wave of his hand.

"It could have been any one of us who found him. I just finally guessed right." As uncomfortable as her compliment made him, at least she wasn't wasting more energy blaming herself for an incident she could have done nothing to change.

"You did more than that. You took charge of our search party and made sure we covered the whole village. You made sure everyone stayed in contact by phone. You even tried to get inside my son's head, so you could figure out where he'd gone."

"That's all just basic police work. Any trooper out of the training program would have done the same."

Tricia's lips turned up at that, the first time she'd smiled all night. Brett didn't know what he'd done to deserve that, but he'd do it a hundred more times if only it could keep her smiling.

"Learn to take a compliment, will you?"

"Thank you. But I just wanted you to know I didn't do anything so amazing. Anyone could have—"

"Brett." If her speaking his name hadn't stopped him, the fact that she'd just set both hands on his shoulders, the warmth of her touch seeping through his henley shirt, would have done it. "Not just anyone would have come out in the middle of the night to help me find my little boy. Not just anyone would have had the skills to find him, even if he did. And if that person had been fortunate enough to find my troubled child, not everyone would have reached out to him the way you did.''

He shook his head, the need to press his cheek against the hand still resting on his shoulder pulling at him, threatening to draw him in. ''It's only fishing.''

''It's more than that, and you know it. And I want to thank you for it.''

He had to hope that when she leaned almost imperceptibly toward him that she intended to hug him because his arms went around her so easily. So different from a few moments before when he'd held her close to help her—and him—withstand an onslaught of emotions, this time she felt warm in his arms.

The way their arms and shoulders fit together, as if God had formed each of them to step perfectly into the other's embrace, surprised him almost more than the fact that she was there, her chin resting against his shoulder.

What started as a hug of gratitude had become something more. Neither moved for several seconds. Each had their reasons, he supposed, but his was that the moment was too perfect to spoil with motion. But then he inhaled the floral scent of her hair. In what felt like the most natural action in the world, he bent to kiss the top of her head. Then again at her temple.

Perhaps it was out of surprise that Tricia lifted her head to meet his gaze, but his heart wouldn't allow him time to clarify it as he dipped his head to hers. The moment their lips touched, Brett knew the mistake he'd made. Even if he never kissed her again in this lifetime, he'd never wake another morning without missing the joy of touching her sweet, soft mouth.

He pulled away so he could see her lovely porcelain doll face. Her eyes were wide, and her bottom lip trembled, but still her hands slid from his shoulders to clasp behind his neck. He'd never felt so unworthy. That she possibly welcomed his kiss both frightened and thrilled him.

Unable to stop himself, he pressed his lips to hers just once more, but this time he gave her his heart with the kiss. Only with reluctance could he pull away. He was on a crash course to heartbreak as she'd probably never be able to return his feelings, but he couldn't stop or change direction.

If only he could have held onto his heart, could have chosen a safer place to share it. But even he could see that it was far too late for him to protect it. His heart was no longer his to give.

It was hers.

Chapter Twelve

"Uh...Brett...I think it's time for you to go home."

Tricia whispered the words with lips still only a breath away from Brett's. With a mouth that still tingled with the memory of a kiss she should have never allowed, much less wish to be repeated. Slowly, she unlaced her fingers behind his neck, as if he wouldn't notice now that she'd clasped them there to draw him to her.

Brett cleared his throat and stepped back from her. "Yeah, I guess I'd better."

He had a shell-shocked expression that mirrored her feelings inside—a battle waged and lost. But when she expected him to look away, to study a spot on the wall like she was tempted to do, he continued to stare at her. What did he see? She wondered if he could see her confusion, her fear. Did he understand she hadn't kissed any man since Rusty left for work that day... that last day?

She'd expected fear the first time she allowed another man to kiss her, and she hadn't been disappointed. Kissing Brett had been terrifying, like diving into a pool with her eyes closed and only praying for water. The strange thing was she'd also expected to feel guilt that first time, the same kind she'd felt every time she'd gone on a date, as if she were betraying her wedding vows. As if she still could. But in Brett's arms, she'd only felt warm and...right. That was the scariest thing of all.

Brett lowered his gaze to the hands she'd been wringing together, and then glanced at the front door. "Okay, I'm going."

"Thanks for coming," she said automatically. Then she stopped herself. No trite send-off comment would ever be acceptable for Brett. "Thanks for bringing Rusty, Jr. back to me."

He raised an eyebrow at her obvious avoidance of the subject that still dangled heavily between them. "I wanted to do it. I'm glad he's okay."

The proverbial elephant sat in the middle of the living room. Were they both going to ignore its presence to save themselves the embarrassment of talking about it? No, she'd avoided enough subjects tonight. "Brett, about...you know...what happened, I don't know what I was thinking. I'm sure you'll agree, it was a mistake."

"You mean the kiss?"

She could only nod to answer him, her cheeks warming under his perusal. It didn't seem possible that the monumentally distressing event could be boiled down to a single word, but Brett had managed it. Such a small word for something that had reawakened the passionate side of her, the personal side, that she'd believed to have died with Rusty. She was troubled, realizing how easily Brett had roused her from that sleep.

His voice was soft as he spoke again. "I'm not sorry. I'd been thinking about kissing you for a long time."

She swallowed. "Oh."

She wouldn't lie and say she'd been thinking about it, too. Her energy had been too focused on not feeling anything, not letting anyone get close enough to hurt her. Brett tempted her to toss away those safeguards and experience her buried feelings fully. She wasn't ready for that—it was too much to ask of her fragile heart.

Taking a deep breath, she dove in. "You know as well as anybody that I'm not ready for any kind of serious relationship. I don't know when, if ever, I'll be ready to move on."

"I'm not asking for a relationship."

That was what she'd wanted him to say, so why did her chest ache with disappointment when he spoke the words? But he'd kissed her. He'd held her in his arms, absorbing her misery. Had he only been offering comfort, and she'd mistaken it for something more tender?

And an even bigger question—did she want something precious from him? Because the answer to that question incriminated her, she refused to answer it, even to herself.

"What are you asking for?" Even she could hear the frustration in her voice.

"I want us to go on dates, plural."

"Brett, we've talked about this before, and—"

"Rusty, Jr. approves."

Tricia drew in sharp breath. "You heard that?" If he did hear, just how long had he been listening through the door? Long enough to hear her son ask if Brett was her boyfriend?

"I heard."

Still, she shook her head, the last remnants of her resistance linking arms and forming a protective blockade around her heart. "It's probably a mistake."

"And you won't know whether it is or not unless you give it a shot." He tilted his head the way her children did to plead their case in the grocery store candy aisle. "Even Rusty, Jr.'s willing to give me a chance as his fishing partner and as a guy for his mother. How about you? Will you give me a chance?"

Tricia would have said she had nothing to lose if it were the truth. She and her children had *everything* to lose if she made a mistake. And it probably was one. But she was tired of coming up with reasons to keep her distance from Brett Lancaster, not when she enjoyed being with him so much. When her children liked him so much. Sure, her fears still mattered but not enough to stop her this time.

"Yes, I'll go out with you again. But it won't be anything serious, right?"

"Of course not." Brett breathed out an exaggerated sigh and winked at her. "Whew, I thought I was going to have to get down and beg. Thanks for saving me from that."

Her laughter felt good in her lungs. Freeing. "You mean if I waited just a few minutes longer…?"

"Never said I wouldn't try everything else I could think of first."

"Well," she said, shrugging. "Okay, then."

With a glance at his watch, Brett started backing toward the door. "I'm going. Really, this time."

"So, you'll call me then?"

He shook his head and chuckled. "Now she gets anxious. Go figure." But he met her gaze and held it. "Count on it. I'll schedule with Rusty, Jr., too."

Following him, she stood in the doorway as he stepped onto the porch. "Drive safely."

"I always do." With a wave, Brett descended the steps and went down the walk. Near to the sidewalk, he turned and glanced back at her. "If it was this hard to convince you to date me, I can't imagine how hard it's going to be if I propose someday."

Brett continued to his car, climbed in and pulled away. Good thing for her he didn't glance back because he would have found her standing there, her mouth gaping.

The spring chill seeping through her light sweater, she returned inside and locked the door. *If I propose someday.* Obviously, he'd meant it as a joke, and he certainly had the right to find it funny, considering the hoops he'd had to jump through before she agreed to date him. So if she'd gotten the punch line, then why were her nerve endings springing up in warning, as if she'd just brushed too close to a flame? He hadn't even said *when.* Only *if.* But realizing that it might be in the realm of possibility—anywhere beyond absolutely not—bewildered her.

The idea that Brett's intentions concerning her could be more serious than he'd let on was even more unsettling. She tried to tell herself it was impossible, but she didn't have to be a cop to see evidence that said the opposite. He'd continually placed himself in her line of vision. He'd refused to be pressed in Julia's direction, and yet he'd still willingly attended a church singles group. Okay, it was possible. Probable.

If she had any sense, she would renege on the whole dating plan before it was too late. She was just fooling herself. It had been too late the moment she'd sat beside Brett at Joe Louis Arena and had the time of her life.

Now she was worried about how to let him down easy, how to protect him from the heartbreak she was sure to give him eventually. But the situation was becoming so unclear. She wanted Brett around—but not too close. She looked forward to dating him—but only if their relationship didn't get too warm. Suddenly, all of the effort seemed futile, dishonest even. Whose heart was she protecting, his or hers?

Sounds of bickering and fidgeting in the back seat tried to drown out the Christian music filtering from the CD player, and someone kept kicking the back of his seat, but Brett refused to become frustrated. Today was just another nearly perfect day in a series of nearly perfect days the last four weeks since Tricia had agreed to date him.

It didn't matter that their dates usually required a table for five instead of two. He loved being with Tricia's children. Today he wouldn't let himself wish for more. But he was a man. Who could blame him for wanting to be alone with Tricia, to hold her the way he had just once? He would never tire of holding her.

"Mommy, he's touching me," Max announced in a screeching voice that would grate on the nerves of far better men than Brett.

"Well, he keeps trying to put his feet on the hump," Rusty, Jr. shouted back. "It's my turn."

Brett wanted to yell a little himself, about how Max's feet couldn't even reach the center hump from his perch in the booster car seat, but Tricia only laughed at their squabbling. The tinkling sound transformed the car's interior from chaotic to calm.

"Hey guys, Mr. Brett isn't going to take us to the movies anymore if we fight the whole way there."

"When can we go fishing again?" Rusty, Jr. asked.

Brett could almost hear the smile in the boy's voice.

Already they'd gone together three times, but Rusty, Jr. couldn't get enough of using his new casting skill. "Why don't we take Lani and Max next time?"

Rusty, Jr. grunted. "If we have to."

"Not today, though," Lani announced. "I can't wait to see the movie. Can we have popcorn *and* candy, Mr. Brett? Mom only lets us have popcorn."

"I guess that's up to your mom." He gave the passenger next to him a sidelong glance.

To a chorus of "Please, Mom's," she finally agreed to sugar and salt.

"Go, Mom. Go, Mom," the trio chanted, complete with a seated happy dance.

Brett might have joined in, too, if not for the scene ahead of him on the interstate, still a few miles from the Novi exit and their movie megaplex destination. The accident appeared to have just happened—some idiot trying to make an illegal U-turn on one of the gravel drives marked "for service vehicles only." The genius must have nearly stopped to make that dangerous maneuver, giving a big surprise to the driver behind him who couldn't stop.

"Hey kids, I might have to give you a rain check on the movie," he said, pulling his SUV next to the highway's cement divider and slowing to a stop.

Tricia lifted an eyebrow. "Aren't you off duty?"

Brett spread his hands outward to explain. "State Police troopers are first responders. That means we're required to stop at accident scenes, no matter where we are in Michigan. Sometimes it's a pain.'' He turned and grinned at the children. ''Like now.''

Lani sat forward in the seat, craning her neck to get a better look. ''Can we watch?''

He grabbed his cell phone and opened the driver's side door just enough for him to slip out. ''Only from inside this car, okay?''

All three children nodded.

Brett jogged along the paved median as traffic blew past them, the force rattling the car she waited in. She folded her damp hands in her lap, trying not to wring them and alarm the children. One very worried person in the car was plenty. The worst part was knowing that investigating fender benders—he'd called them ''property damage accidents''—was just the mundane daily stuff Brett did. He rarely spoke about more *exciting* parts of his job and tried not to let her catch him adjusting his ankle holster for the gun he always carried. She appreciated his thoughtfulness.

''Mommy, do you think there'll be a big shoot-out?'' Rusty, Jr. asked with glee in his voice.

''Or maybe there'll be a big drug bust, and Mr. Brett's picture will be on the front page,'' Lani chimed.

''I doubt there'll be a shoot-out or any drug arrests. But if you guys think so, I'll have to wonder if you're watching too much TV.''

If she was so convinced, then why had her hands turned icy cold? Her stomach rolled. She could see that front page, too. The headline would read something like, "Off-Duty Trooper Another Casualty in Drug War." Along with his state police portrait, a sub-headline probably would say, "Girlfriend/children witnessed brutal slaying."

No, she was letting her imagination get the best of her again. Until now, she'd contained her worries so well that she could even ask him about his day without cringing. She had to be stronger if she planned on spending so much time with Brett, and she'd stopped lying to herself by saying that wasn't what she wanted.

From one of the two crumpled cars blocking the eastbound lanes, two hysterical teenage girls emerged. An overall-clad man climbed out of the other.

"No, Mommy. Not too much TV," Max supplied for the three of them.

"Are you sure? I have to protect you from seeing too much TV violence. That's *my* job." But it wasn't television she worried about right now. Had her newly purchased police scanner and her secret habit of listening to it whenever Brett was on patrol contributed to their imaginative stories? She tried to listen only when they were outside playing or at school, but they could have overheard a few times.

Lani let out an exasperated sigh. "We're sure, Mom. We almost never see TV violence. *Veggie Tales* doesn't have much violence—like a blueberry beating a tomato and making sauce or something."

Tricia had to laugh at her clever daughter who was grinning at her when she pulled down the visor mirror to check her lipstick. She flipped it back up to see

Brett taking charge of the chaotic situation. He didn't require his uniform to put on the command-bearing demeanor the impossibly young girls were responding to. Her children still chattered in the back as they watched the exciting event unfold, but Tricia no longer paid attention as she watched Brett at work.

Pride, not fear, welled in her chest as she watched him meld authority and compassion in a way that convinced the girls, uninjured except for a few scrapes and bruises, to stop sobbing and to begin explaining how the accident had happened, which they did with exaggerated hand motions.

It couldn't have been more clear to her that God had led Brett to his line of work, had formed him to handle the stress and respond with quiet authority instead of a show of force. His training had only reinforced qualities he already possessed. Though she had no doubt Brett could get tough when he had to, especially when one of his fellow troopers was in trouble, he didn't hide behind that mask.

Within a few minutes, a patrol car pulled up on the shoulder of the highway, passing the line of cars backed up behind the accident scene. Another state trooper, this one in uniform, took charge of the situation, radioing for a paramedic to examine the teenage driver and her passenger.

For a moment, Tricia felt as if she was just meeting the man she'd come to care so much about for the first time, but then she realized she'd known him all along.

The honor, the trust, the dignity—they'd always been there. They just came along with a badge.

Brett was who he was, and she didn't want to change a thing about him. Somehow she had to force herself to overcome her fears about the life he led when they were apart—they were her problem, not his. Only when she did that could she fully enjoy spending time with him.

She wasn't sure where their relationship would lead, but she knew one thing. Her life and the lives of her children were better with Brett Lancaster in them.

"Who knew popcorn could multiply like this?"

Brett laughed out loud as he crawled on the living room floor a few hours later, picking up as many popcorn kernels as possible. Tricia and the children were doing the same, but it appeared only the grown-ups were making much headway in the mess while the youngsters seemed to drop as much as they shot in the trash can. The hardest part was separating the popcorn kernels from the game pieces—some big and plastic, some tiny and metal—also littering the floor.

Tricia grinned at him. "It's one of the many mysteries of parenting. Just like why a chocolate bar never divides in three equal pieces." She lifted the sofa cushion and shoved several unpopped kernels in the trash.

"Save some for carpet mites. They're hungry, too."

"I'm sure they're chunky bugs at our house. Especially after tonight."

Brett smiled back at her. It had been another great night, even if the accident had made them miss the movie. At least after he'd been able to make himself stop watching Tricia, expecting to see her panicked expression. Though he'd worried they would be back to zero again in his effort to increase her comfort level, she'd appeared oddly serene, as if danger no longer bothered her.

She'd even surprised him by jumping at his suggestion of buying real movie popcorn and drugstore candy and taking the children back to the house to play board games.

Max leaned his nose next to the tan pile carpet. "What are carpet mites, Mommy?"

"Believe me, you don't want to know." Tricia rubbed her hand along his cheek.

"Do you think they'll eat Mr. Plum or the candlestick?" the boy asked, holding up both.

Brett sauntered over to the two of them and ruffled the boy's hair. "Not if you return them and the confidential file back to the box right away. But little boys who stay up too late—"

Tricia pulled her eyebrows together in a frown. "Brett Lancaster, don't you scare him before bed." Then she turned back to her son. "No, honey, carpet mites don't nibble on children, even yummy ones."

Brett did his best to look offended. "Before I was so rudely interrupted, I was about to say those little boys turn to sugar so they could be gobbled up by grown-ups."

"Oh, that's *much* better." But her son scrambled away from her so he could pretend to fight off being eaten by the monster grown-up.

Pretty soon two reinforcements joined the battle, hauling Brett to the floor and drawing in their mother for good measure, until a giggling mass of bodies looked like a game of Twister gone bad. As much as he would have enjoyed being alone with Tricia, this was better. Real. This was the family he very much wanted to be a part of, no matter how long he had to wait for it.

But was it real when he had to be carefully vague to Tricia about his shifts to prevent that wary look from filtering into her eyes? Would he ever be able to be open with her, honest about that part of him that was so inextricably tied to his identity that he couldn't separate the two?

As he lay on his back, trapped under three junior-size bodies, his hand somehow found Tricia's, and their fingers entwined. A trap of his own making—he felt it close over him then, pressing the air from his lungs. A more noble man would have bowed out gracefully long ago, unwilling to subject Tricia to the uncertainties of his life when she'd already suffered loss. Or he'd walk away from his career in favor of some staid office job—or, worse yet, a family business that gave him no joy.

But he was neither noble nor unselfish. He'd already proved that. As much as he didn't want to lose her, he also couldn't give up his identity for anyone a second time. And there didn't seem to be any graceful exit from this relationship now that he recognized he was in love with her. The reality hadn't struck like a lightning bolt the way it did in the movies. It had come in baby steps and in small awakenings—the sound of her voice, the generosity of her heart, the smell of her hair, the sweet way she nurtured her children.

And then here he was, on the brink of disaster, regretting and not regretting at the same time. He couldn't let her go. What was he going to do now?

Nothing tonight, he realized with relief. Gently rolling little bodies off him, he sat up and shoved his hand back through his hair. "I don't know about you guys, but I'm real tired."

"Will we see you tomorrow, Mr. Brett?" Lani asked.

He lifted an eyebrow at Tricia. Saturday was supposed to be a date where it was just the two of them, alone. He'd been looking forward to it, and now it seemed like something that would only be sweet torture.

"You will for a few minutes." She paused to a chorus of whines before continuing. "You'll be spending the night with Rick and Charity." Those whines turned to cheers.

"So I'll see you tomorrow." By turns, he ruffled each of the children's hair and then kissed them atop their heads. When he reached Tricia, he didn't stop to second-guess himself. He placed a chaste but sweet kiss on her cheek. His lips tingled with the memory of kissing her lips as he lingered, just a breath away from that precious prize. A breath caught in his throat as he backed away, watching her eyes go wide.

"Ew, Mr. Brett kissed Mommy," Rusty, Jr. announced as if any of them had missed it.

Max's reaction came in a single word, "Yuck," while Lani only showed a small smile, as if she knew a wonderful secret and might share.

Tricia only stared at the carpet, her cheeks flushing prettily. She wouldn't meet his gaze. Was she trying to tell him something? He knew she cared about him. He'd seen the tender way she looked at him when they were playing in the backyard with her children. Was that it? Did she just care for him as a dear friend who'd been kind to her children?

The thought that she might not love him, might never be able to return his feelings, suddenly weighed heavily on his shoulders, making him tired.

So it was with false cheerfulness that he waved to everyone and headed out the door. The thought struck him again that his loving might not be enough. He'd known from the start what he was up against. But he only smiled grimly into the darkness. Even if she'd signed a document the day they had met and had it notarized, saying she would never want him, that she could never be with him, he'd still be in this same predicament now. Because from the beginning his heart had begged to be near her.

Chapter Thirteen

This was the night he'd been waiting for, Brett reminded himself Saturday as he sat on one end of the sofa with Tricia curled up on the other and a huge popcorn bowl nestled between them. But this wasn't exactly how he'd imagined it, with enough space between them to easily fit at least…oh…three small children.

Tricia stared at the screen where a horrible kung fu action flick played on the VCR. She wasn't watching the movie any more than he was. And if she was even half as nervous as he was, she would probably have come out of her skin if he so much as poked her.

"Tell me again why you picked this movie."

She chuckled as he'd hoped she would and uncurled her legs from beneath the skirt of the emerald-colored knit dress that seemed to create specks of color in her dark eyes. Small stocking-clad feet, with burgundy-painted toenails, settled on the floor in front of the couch. "I didn't want you to be able to say I only choose chick flicks."

"No, I couldn't say that. You picked a guy movie, all right, but did you have to go for subtitles, too?"

"That was just a bonus."

She laughed again, finally appearing relaxed. Maybe now he could lighten up, too. It wasn't as if they'd never been alone together before. There was the time at the hockey game—if you could call being surrounded by an arena full of other hockey fans alone. After the singles group event. That picnic in her backyard. The night when they'd lost—and found—her son.

The night they'd kissed.

He could forget trying to relax. Because tonight was different than any of those other times. It was even different from all the dates they'd been on in the last few weeks with the whole gang. This time, not only was it just the two of them, but the tête-à-tête was planned. Oh, and did he mention that it was just the two of them?

Again, Tricia curled her legs under the protective hem of her dress. "Do you think the kids are all right with Rick and Charity? I should probably call—"

"Tricia, they're fine. You know they are. And if they weren't, Charity knows the number."

"Yeah, you're right."

"But I hate to tell you this…" He paused until she met his gaze, appearing confused. "This movie is not fine. Do you have anything else? Or do we have to go back to the video store?''

Brett walked to the television stand and picked up the two black video containers on top. ''Elvis Presley?''

Tricia covered her face with both hands and giggled like the girl she probably had been when she started watching these B-movies with their hokey singer-gets-the-girl plots. He wished he'd known her then, before life had kicked her in the head and made her afraid of living fully. Before she'd become an old spirit in a lovely young form.

Pulling her hands away from her face, she grinned. ''Okay, you found my secret habit. I love those old movies, when every problem can be healed with a love song.''

He removed the distasteful video from the VCR and replaced it with the unusual one. Then, when he turned back to her, he stretched his hands wide and started singing. '''Love me—'''

She popped off the couch and held a hand up to stop him before he even got the ''tender'' out. ''Brett, give the song a break. No problems can be solved with that sound.''

He threw his head back and laughed. ''So you think I shouldn't quit my day job?''

Until it was out of his mouth, he didn't even realize what a loaded question he'd asked. But she surprised him by nodding.

"Someone has to make sure no one lets you loose on the music industry."

"Well, at least you have sound reasons for your opinion. Now we have a very important film to watch."

Just as the "King of Rock 'n' Roll" started crooning his first ballad, Brett returned to the sofa. But this time instead of sitting on his end, he picked up the popcorn bowl and seated himself in its place, resting the bowl in his lap. "Now that's better."

Though he'd said it, he wasn't convinced it was better. From this distance, he could smell the floral shampoo that had captured his senses the moment he'd met her. Lately it lulled him to sleep at night and filtered through his thoughts in his waking hours.

Being this close to her only made him want to touch. Would it be too much too soon? He'd almost talked himself into keeping his hands clasped together until the day he died as long as he could stay near her, when Tricia leaned forward, resting her elbows on her knees and her head in the cradle formed by her hands.

"This is hard, isn't it?" She straightened and pushed her hand back through her hair, which she'd worn loose at her shoulders tonight. "I don't know what I'm doing."

"It's harder without the kids here, isn't it?"

She nodded. "Maybe it's a bad idea for us to be alone. Maybe this whole thing…"

He couldn't let her finish, not when what she was about to say could only hurt him. "Is that what you really want, Tricia? To walk away from this possibility?'' He looked down to see that he'd closed his fingers over her wrist. ''Because I really want to be with you. I've looked forward to being alone with you, so I could do this.''

Her eyes widened with the recognition that he was about to kiss her, but she didn't shake her head or raise her hand to stop him. The enormity of the moment stalled him but not for long, as he leaned in and pressed his lips to hers. She was so warm, so soft. He longed for more than he knew was right, but held his wayward thoughts in check, cherishing the sweetness of Tricia's kiss.

Then, with more strength than he knew he possessed, Brett turned his mouth away from hers until it brushed only her cheek. But the woman who already possessed his heart clung to him, as if craving the comfort of his arms. It should have seemed like the most wonderful gift, but he suspected his were only a replacement for the arms she really wanted to cradle her.

That truth nearly killed him. He'd thought it would be enough to take whatever feelings Tricia could spare for him, but he'd been wrong. Very wrong. He wanted more of her heart. All of it. For that reason, as gently as he could, Brett rested his hands on her shoulders and set her away from him.

''I'll never be a good replacement for him. Are you kissing me or just a ghost from your past? I want— No, I *need* for it to be about me…not him.''

She opened her mouth as if to refute what he'd said, but then she shut it again, pressing her lips together. Her eyes started filling. Without words, she'd confirmed his suspicion.

She wouldn't meet his gaze, so he waited, his heart splintering like shards of blown glass—so tiny but so deadly. What he had to say was too important to be directed at the top of her head.

"Tricia, look at me…please." Again, he waited, but this time she stopped staring at her wringing hands and finally faced him. "You need to understand. All of this—us—isn't casual for me anymore. Maybe it never was."

A single tear escaped her battle to contain them, and automatically he reached over to brush it away. He could deny her nothing, and he knew it. He should have stopped talking. It would be easier on the both of them if he could. But the words burned within him until he could bear it no more.

"I'm in love with you."

Tricia stared at the frothy bubbles in the sink as she washed the popcorn bowl and glasses. In each of the sparkling larger bubbles, she saw Brett's face as he confessed the words she couldn't quite reconcile. In the slurp of the draining water, she heard the hopelessness in his voice.

I'm in love with you. How could she digest that knowledge? It terrified her, demanded feelings from her that she'd thought long dead. But that part of her heart reserved for loving, mature relationships was very much alive, she'd discovered. Now she needed to decide what to do with that knowledge.

Brett had misunderstood her reaction. And her silence had done little to clear up his mistake. How could she explain to him the shame she'd felt? Her thoughts hadn't been about Rusty at all. She'd promised to love that man all the days of her life, and yet in Brett's comforting arms, she'd forgotten all about him. As if he'd never existed, never mattered. How could she have forgotten?

Yes, she'd reached out to Brett but not as a substitute, the way he'd suspected. As soon as his arms had encircled her, she'd realized how much she craved the peace she'd found there.

He loved her. The fact didn't frighten her as much as it first had. Sure, the idea would take some getting used to, but this was Brett she was talking about. Brett, the man who was generous to a fault, chivalrous in a day when few still valued that quality, heroic without even trying. He hadn't demanded that she return his love, or even seemed to expect that she could.

Her heart squeezed over the hopelessness he must have felt. She'd once felt that way, too, as if the tunnel she was crawling through on her hands and knees had no light at its end…only an endless stretch of tunnel.

She wasn't ready to admit it to him, but Brett had helped her to see that first flicker of light. Though it was only a match with a tiny and temporary flame at first, it offered the possibility for a bright beacon later.

She was grateful to him for being her friend. She'd discouraged his friendship at every step, yet he'd returned again and again. Why he'd tried so hard, she couldn't imagine. Somewhere along the way, her resolve and her heart had softened.

Brett wanted more than friendship from her, but she was terrified to take that step—that attempt at skydiving without a parachute. She wasn't ready. Wasn't sure when she would be.

But there was one thing she was ready for, even if it had taken her much too long to reach this point. She would finally be the kind of friend to Brett that he'd been to her. She wanted to make good on her plan to help him heal his wounded heart and to rediscover his faith.

She wanted him to know joy, even if she wasn't ready to be a part of his life. She needed that for him. Did he even realize something was missing in his heart? She certainly hadn't realized what she was missing in her tunnel, so she doubted he did.

Tricia dried her hands on the towel and shut off the kitchen light, listening to the strange house sounds on this first night when she'd been truly alone in years. She missed the rustling noises of restless young sleepers, the steady rhythm of their nighttime breathing. There were other sounds and sights she missed as well as she passed through the darkened living room on the way to bed. She missed the hearty cadence of Brett's laughter, his ready smile. Even the way he ate popcorn one fluffy kernel at a time instead of grabbing a handful and crunching on it the way her children did.

Yes, Brett loved her. If she were honest with herself, she would admit she loved him, too.

Laughter and chatter filled the classroom of the family life center as nearly two dozen adults lined the U-shaped arrangement of tables, Reverend Bob standing at the opening. Brett glanced about the crowd that was decidedly female except for him, the church's two ministers and the blond guy from the singles group.

The young guy, who appeared to hang on Hannah's every word, obviously was here to score points with her. So what was *his* excuse? Before Brett had a chance to contemplate that question, Reverend Bob raised his hands to silence the class.

"Good morning, everyone. I'm glad so many of you could make it. For those of you who are attending for the first time, you've picked a great day for it."

Great day? Through the classroom window, the sky appeared gray with the threat of a May downpour instead of the flowers the old rhyme always promised. If the sun felt as surly as he did this morning, it would refuse to shine for weeks.

Out of the corner of his eye, he watched Tricia, her gaze transfixed on her minister. Still, the way she steadied her hands on the table in front of her revealed that she knew he was watching. Was she also feeling guilty for using his fragile heart to trick him into coming with her to Bible study? *She ought to be.*

He turned his gaze forward again, only to find most of the class watching him and then nodding a greeting after they'd finally caught his eye. He waved first to Hannah and then at Charity who, surprisingly, sat next to her infamous mother, Laura Sims. More surprising, Julia sat on Charity's opposite side.

Tricia had explained to him that though Mrs. Sims had caused a scandal by pretending she was a widow rather than a divorcée, she still sanctimoniously avoided situations where she would have to face Charity's sister, refusing to accept the child of her ex-husband and his second wife.

"I'd like to welcome Brett Lancaster, Tricia Williams, Grant Sumner and Olivia Wells to our class today," Reverend Bob continued.

After several hellos, Brett glanced at Tricia again, and this time she met his gaze and smiled. He tried to ignore the fluttering in his stomach that soon would transform into a dull ache. He would have to get used to ignoring a lot of things about Tricia if they were going to be just friends as she so obviously wished. Otherwise, why would she have brought him here?

When she'd asked him if he was free Wednesday morning on his day off, he'd hoped she was planning a breakfast date where she would finally confess her feelings for him. Instead, she'd invited him to go with her to Bible study, an outing that had "I want us to be friends" written all over it.

Because watching her only made him angrier, Brett glanced toward the other new attendees. Grant seemed nice enough, moving about the room and shaking hands with everyone. An attractive middle-aged woman, Olivia appeared more reserved, smiling at those who greeted her but quickly returning her attention to the front of the class. Something about her sun-streaked, short blond hair and carefully applied makeup looked familiar. She might have attended the singles group meetings like Grant had, though Brett couldn't say for sure.

Whether he'd seen her before or not, Brett didn't have to wonder what—or, rather, who—had inspired Olivia to seek out Scripture study that morning. She appeared only to have eyes for Reverend Bob. The minister's nervous smile hinted that he, too, had noticed the woman's vibe and was secretly pleased by it. *You go, Reverend.* From the look of the minister and his daughter, at least a few people appeared to be winning in this singles game.

Clearing his throat, Reverend Bob continued his introduction with an excitement reserved for history teachers in their Civil War discussions. "We've just completed our study of the Book of Luke, so we're taking a breather this week before we delve into Paul's letter to the church at Ephesus, or the Book of Ephesians."

"So, what are we going to look at today? Song of Solomon?" Andrew asked, his grin suggesting he, too, had noticed the interesting development in his boss's love life.

Reverend Bob chuckled, a blush crawling up his

neck at Andrew's suggestion of the Bible's most sensual book. Then he shook his head. "Perhaps another day. Today I thought we'd look in Ecclesiastes, at a passage you should all find familiar."

Despite his obvious discomfort, the minister took hold of his Bible, placed his finger slightly past the middle and popped the book open, just like Brett remembered doing during Bible drills when he was a child. When church was still exciting. When he still trusted God to make everything in his life okay.

"Please turn your Bibles to chapter three. Serena, could you read beginning at verse one?"

After a flutter of pages, Andrew's wife started reading. "'For everything there is a season, and a time for every matter under heaven: a time to be born, and a time to die...'"

Brett's thoughts traveled as the young mother read on through the planting and the plucking of the planted things, through the killing and healing, the mourning and dancing. He'd been convinced that Tricia's time to mourn had ended, and he wanted to be her partner when she was ready to dance. But she appeared no more ready to move on with her life than when he'd first met her. Maybe he'd just been kidding himself all along.

Serena's words invaded his thoughts as she read on.

"'A time to embrace, and a time to refrain from embracing; a time to seek, and a time to lose...'"

Would his time with Tricia ever come? Would he ever hold her in his arms and be certain it was *his* comfort she craved? He'd sought her out, offering friendship and more, but he sensed that though she welcomed his friendship, it was still his time to lose someone he'd grown to love more than he'd ever loved Claire.

He wondered now if he'd ever loved Claire, or just the idea of her, a suitable match and his partner in ministry. The image never would have been enough to base a life on, but with Tricia, it was so different. His first thoughts in the morning and his last thoughts at night were of her welfare, her peace of mind, her broken heart.

His need to protect her, to be a part of her life and that of her children overwhelmed all thoughts of his own needs, though he recognized that his happiness also hinged on all of those things.

Lord, I don't understand Your purpose here. Did You lead me to Tricia so that I would learn humility? I've got that down now, so can we go on to something else. Strange, but he felt the need to lean on God in a way that he hadn't for a long time. He was a capable man. It was so easy for him to be self-reliant, especially while questioning a faith he'd not been able to separate from Claire.

He'd chosen to stand alone, instead of opening himself up to God. But he didn't want to stand alone anymore. He was calling on the Father here, and the relationship felt so intimate, the way he remembered it. Just the two of them. It had nothing to do with the relationship he'd built and lost in his youth or with anything he dreamed of one day having with Tricia, though he hoped God would be at the center of that, too.

"Isn't it comforting to know that God has a plan for our lives?" Reverend Bob asked after Serena stopped reading. "'To every time, there is a season.' Yes, friends, God is in control."

Brett jerked. Was Reverend Bob talking to him? That message sure sounded as if he'd been its target. But from the nods he saw and the amens he heard, he guessed that the Scripture had spoken to others as well.

"So, Reverend Bob, what do we as Christians do when our time isn't God's time?" Andrew lifted an eyebrow, and the rest of the class chuckled with him.

It was the question of the hour. Brett wasn't sure he could survive waiting for God to iron out this wrinkled mess with Tricia, but he was willing to try.

"Well, Andrew, I think we pray a lot about it," Reverend Bob answered with a smile. "And then we can look up Isaiah 40:31 and start memorizing it. It begins, 'But they that wait upon the Lord shall renew their strength.'"

Finished kidding his boss, Andrew piped in with the second line, "'They shall mount up with wings as eagles.'"

Reverend Bob glanced about the room, as if he expected someone to come through with the end of the verse.

Tricia surprised Brett by being the one to do it.

"'They shall run, and not be weary; and they shall walk, and not faint.'"

But she wore an unreadable expression when he turned to face her. She shook her head as if she'd surprised herself as well by coming up with the verse.

The discussion of the passage in Ecclesiastes and the second one in Isaiah continued, but Brett didn't feel comfortable contributing. All that had happened today was too private. He needed to get used to the changes in his heart before he was ready to share them with others.

Chapter Fourteen

Brett was relieved as they filed out of church an hour later, his thoughts still reeling.

"Well, that was different," Tricia said on their way to Brett's car.

Different? That didn't begin to describe either the event that he'd at first hoped would be a date or the way God had chosen to speak to him through the study. "I was mad at you for tricking me into going."

"I'm sorry."

At least she didn't deny it. That would have been too much to take.

"Are you still mad?"

He thought about it for a few seconds. As much as he wanted to stay mad at her, he couldn't. No matter what Tricia's motivation for getting him here, God had used the opportunity to speak to his heart. "No, I'm not."

"I'm glad."

But something about what she'd said a few minutes before didn't sit right with him. "What was different about it? You didn't expect candlelight and romance at Bible study, did you?" Okay, so he wasn't completely over his anger.

She shook her head. "All of this was supposed to be for you."

"For me?"

"Coming here. To Bible study. I wanted to do it for you, so you could remember the reason you gave your life to God in the first place."

His breath caught in his throat before he forcibly released it. They'd talked about their faith before. It wasn't so amazing that she'd guessed, yet he still was surprised that she had. "Why would you do that?"

"I want you to have joy. How long has it been since you've felt any joy in your faith? You just seem to be going through the motions of faith, and I wanted more for you. A lot more."

Again, he studied her, ignoring the seed of hope threatening to sprout inside his mind. That she was concerned about the status of his soul didn't automatically follow that she was in love with him, but he couldn't help wishing it was that easy.

Because it wasn't, he squeezed her arm gently before opening her car door. "Thanks." Then he remembered. "Wait, it was *supposed* to be for me?"

She looked up at him as she settled in the car, her expression sad. "Why was it so easy to see it in you when I couldn't see it in myself?"

As he crossed to his side of the car and sat, he pondered her words until recognition dawned. "You mean going through the motions?" He waited for her nod. "It's easy to do, isn't it? To get up every day and believe the way you always have but to keep God at arms' length."

Brett put the car in Drive and pulled out of the church lot. Just when he'd determined that they were in agreement, Tricia started shaking her head.

"But I can no longer do that. The motions aren't enough anymore. The Scriptures today seemed as if they were written just for me."

"You, too, huh? Is that why you had such a strange expression when you were quoting that verse?"

The side of her mouth turned up. "I kept hearing those verses about a time for this and a time for that, and it seemed like God was asking, 'Isn't it about time for you to return to Me?'"

"Wow, God was really working the room this morning. And I thought He was focusing on getting me to quit my lonely martyr routine." He paused for a few seconds and then added, "He convinced me."

He was glad for the stoplight at Hickory Ridge Road and General Motors Road because once their eyes met, he wasn't sure he could have turned his attention back to the road. He only wanted to keep looking at her and watching her meet his gaze just as steadily. They seemed to have connected on a deeper level than just as man and woman now—bonding as a brother and sister in their faith.

"Um, Brett, the light's green."

The car jerked as he turned to face the road and pressed the accelerator at the same time. A chuckle rose in his throat, and Tricia laughed with him. But when he lowered one hand from the steering wheel, taking hold of hers and lacing their fingers, their laughter stilled. She didn't pull away, her hand warm and comforting.

Brett cleared his throat, ready to open up with her about a subject that until now had felt so private. "Today is the first time the Scriptures have spoken to me in a long time. I felt as if my faith was so tied up in being with Claire that there was nothing left when she was gone."

She was shaking her head no, as if she wanted him to understand how wrong he was. Her compassion only made him want to tell her more.

"But it was all still there," he said. "God was always there, just waiting for me to open up to him again."

She nodded and squeezed his hand. "After Rusty died, I was so busy trying to be self-reliant, to be strong for the children, that I didn't realize I had nothing to prove with God. He was waiting for me, too."

Turning left onto Main Street, they continued driving several minutes in silence. Then Brett blew out a breath. "We certainly are a pair, aren't we?"

Immediately, he was sorry he'd said that. Would she pull away from him? Would the hopelessness return to his heart? He didn't know if they were a pair or if they ever would be. Both had carefully avoided discussing his admission that he loved her. Would they both continue to pretend he'd never said it, that he didn't feel it?

But she only squeezed his hand again and kept her fingers curled over his. The action spoke louder than any verbal answer she could have given.

"Yes." She paused to look over at him. "We are."

His heart must have skipped a beat the way it jolted in his chest. He cautioned himself not to read anything into what she'd said, but the temptation was too great.

Pulling to a stop in front of Tricia's house, he finally lifted his hand away from hers, though it was the last thing he wanted to do. He hoped Mary Nelson, who was watching Max and Rebecca today, had taken the kids out to play in the backyard so he'd have a few more minutes alone with Tricia. There was still so much he needed to hear from her. So much she still hadn't said. He had to believe that.

"I'm glad we did this today," Tricia said, turning toward him.

"Me, too. It sure turned out better than I expected when you tricked me into going."

"I didn't think you'd go if I just asked you."

"You're probably right." He hated that they were back to this—the polite distancing that came after each step they took closer to each other. Not this time. They'd come too far. In his heart, he sensed that she loved him. He could wait for her to realize it, too. But he just couldn't go back.

Yet when she started to speak, he braced his hands on the steering wheel and steadied his heart to be asked to do what he'd just told himself he couldn't.

"Brett, you've been such a great friend to me. Always there, always…"

As her words trailed off, Brett felt his heart begin to splinter. He was a smart guy. He recognized a kiss-off speech when he heard one. But he could take it, he reminded himself, and forced himself to look at her.

Tricia, on the other hand, stared into her lap. "It's just that…I wanted to tell you…I care about you."

He waited for the "but" to come, but it didn't.

"I…" She started again, but whatever she was about to say disappeared when she leaned across the car's console and touched her lips to his. The kiss lasted only a fraction of a second, and it was over.

Still, it was long enough to send Brett's heart into overdrive. Not convinced he wasn't imagining some alternate universe where regular guys like him got the girl, he stared at Tricia, her eyes wide. She was as surprised by the kiss as he was.

What she said next shocked him even more.

"I love you."

It was barely more than a whisper, but she'd said it. He couldn't begin to imagine what it had cost her—admitting what was in her heart. He couldn't fathom the guilt she must have felt over earlier promises she'd made but was no longer under obligation to keep. That only made her confession more precious. He'd never felt more unworthy.

He would have told her all of that, too, if she hadn't lifted the door handle, waved and hurried toward the house. Nothing like dropping a bomb and hightailing it out of there. He waved as she went inside her front door, though he was convinced she wouldn't look back at him.

None of it mattered. She loved him. She'd even said it out loud. Okay, so she'd bailed on him right afterward, but she'd still said it. And she'd kissed him of her own free will. It was enough, at least for now.

She'd kissed him. Kissed *him*. But that adventure in balancing on a cliff's edge hadn't been enough for her. She'd swan dived over the edge by admitting she loved him. The worst part was she didn't regret any of it.

Startled by all that had transpired in those few minutes, Tricia had rushed into the house. Still, she couldn't resist peeking out the living room blind to watch him pull away. She caught sight of him waving, though he probably couldn't have seen her watching.

By contrast, she couldn't have missed seeing the shock on Brett's face when she'd kissed him, or the hope in his eyes that she'd put there. She was tempted to believe that her actions and her words alone had changed everything between them. But she couldn't take that credit. Their relationship's foundation in friendship had already been rocked when Brett had told her how he felt. And even before that, when her feelings had transformed from respecting him as a good person to carrying him in her heart.

Now, though her lungs ached and her hands dampened with anxiety, Tricia didn't want to take back what she'd said. And though she wasn't convinced she was ready to move forward in their relationship, she was positive she didn't want to go back, either. Because in the end, she wanted to be with Brett.

Until that moment, she hadn't really considered it, but now she realized with all her heart that it was true. In the future she'd mentally painted, she'd always pictured herself in the center, flanked by children. But that mental image had changed, the brush strokes creating a place for Brett, next to her, holding her hand.

A smile pulled at her lips as she crossed from the living room to the kitchen, her anxiety transformed into anticipation. She'd barely opened the back door before Max barreled into her arms, Mary and Rebecca following him.

"Hi, Mommy," he said in a muffled voice against her belly. Then he pulled away to look past her. "Where's Mr. Brett? Did he come to play with me?"

"Not this time, sweetheart."

Max already had the refrigerator open and was digging for a snack before he turned back to her. "Is Mr. Brett going to be our new daddy?"

Tricia tried to cover her gasp with a cough. Since Max was still concentrating on his mission of collecting juice boxes for himself and Rebecca, she figured she'd fooled the children, but Mary's knowing smile showed she hadn't been successful all around. After a long pause, she could finally speak. "You have a daddy, Max, even if he is in Heaven."

Rebecca, who seldom said much, chose this moment to speak up. "I don't have a daddy."

Max slurped on his straw. "Mine died. God needed him more than us."

Mary's gaze met with Tricia's and, as if in agreement, each snapped a child she adored into her arms.

"Remember, honey, we all have God as our Father in Heaven," Mary told the tiny towhead she propped on her hip. "And you have Grandpa Bob here on Earth, too."

"Boy, you are lucky," Tricia told Rebecca. "And Max has great grown-up friends like Uncle Rick and Mr. Brett."

"Can Mr. Brett come live with us?" Max asked.

Out of her peripheral vision, Tricia caught Mary trying not to laugh. Finally, she smiled. It wouldn't be anytime soon. A few years from then. And, of course, a wedding ring and a church ceremony would be involved. But, maybe, just maybe Max would get what he'd asked for.

And maybe he wouldn't be the only one to get his wish.

The following Saturday morning, Trooper Joe Rossetti checked the Welch Hitch under the pant leg of his uniform, and automatically Brett bent forward to check his. At least with this leashlike gadget there they'd both be prepared for one possibility—that they could secure the legs of a dirtbag who was trying to kick his way out of the patrol car. Joe sure didn't seem to think Brett was ready for the other plan he had in mind.

"Don't you think you're jumping the gun, pal?" Joe said for the third time as they sat side by side at a pair of PC terminals in the squad room.

Brett sighed as he typed details into an arrest report for a domestic assault case. "I told you, she already said she loved me. What else does she have to say before I pop the question?"

"Your place or hers?" Trooper Rossetti chuckled at his totally inappropriate joke.

Brett didn't laugh because it wasn't funny and didn't backhand him because he usually—although not at this particular moment—valued their friendship. Instead he lowered his voice and growled, "You're talking about my future wife."

"Lighten up, will ya?"

"Only if you back off. You might be able to joke about your…female collection, but we're talking about Tricia here." He didn't have to say he disapproved of Joe's cavalier treatment of women. Nor was it necessary for Brett to tag the phrase, *the woman I love,* after Tricia's name. Both were understood.

Joe shrugged, hardly contrite, and continued typing in his larceny report for another stolen Jet Ski in the annual rash of thefts just before the summer boating season.

"Tricia's been married before, you know."

"But not to me." Brett bristled at the unkind reminder that his would-be bride had been touched before. By her husband. If Joe knew what was good for him, he wouldn't push any further.

Joe patted his shoulder as he stood up from the PC and collected his hat. "You really do love her, don't you?"

Brett nodded, the animosity from a moment before

forgotten. "I can't believe it's tonight." Automatically, he reached in his coat pocket and ran his fingers over the soft-sticky felt box waiting there. Inside it, a simple diamond solitaire awaited Tricia's answer. Could he wait until their date tonight to hear what she would say?

"Don't worry, she'll say yes." Joe watched as his friend withdrew his hand from the coat pocket. "She'll have to after all the trouble you've gone to."

This time, Brett did punch him in the arm. "Thanks for the support, buddy."

"What are friends for? What are you going to use all those church people for?"

Patting the pocket one last time, he stood up and grabbed his hat. "They'll all be waiting at the park for us after we have dinner. I've hired a horse and carriage to drive us through the downtown. We'll end up at Central Park. That's when several church members will surround us and serenade us with love songs."

"How'd you arrange it all in just three days?"

"Charity, a lady from church, helped some, but my sister, Jenny, did the most. She still feels guilty for what she did when she set me up with Tricia, so I let her do some penance."

"You're not sorry she played matchmaker, are you?"

Brett shook his head. "No way. But I needed help, and she still felt guilty, so we helped each other out."

Lieutenant Matt Dawson crossed through the squad room then and stopped behind their desks. "Trooper

Rossetti and Trooper Lancaster. Shouldn't there be a couple more patrol cars on the road about now?''

"On our way, Lieutenant," Joe answered. Still, as he stepped out of the heavy metal door that led to the police car lot, he turned back to Brett. "Sounds like you have it all planned out. Good luck, pal. It will either be a proposal romantic enough for the history books or one they'll write comedy routines about."

"Remind me again, why are we friends?"

Joe winked at him. "Because we'd take a bullet for each other without a second thought, and you know it."

Brett did know that. Just as he was certain he wanted to spend the rest of his life loving Tricia Williams, though he'd prefer her last name be Lancaster.

He wondered how he would be able to make it through the day, waiting to ask her to be his wife. Part of him hoped the rest of the day shift would be slow, so he couldn't get caught up in paperwork and end up working overtime. The other part hoped there'd be at least a little activity to occupy his thoughts.

Either way, it would be the longest day of his life.

Chapter Fifteen

The musical jingle of Saturday morning cartoons drifted into Tricia's bedroom as she stared at the four different outfits spread across her bed. A long skirt and sweater in beige and tan. A bright red blazer and dark slacks. She just knew tonight's date with Brett would be special. The least she could do was look that way when he picked her up, so none of these things would do.

When she'd spoken with him on the phone twice in the three days since she'd confessed her feelings for him, their conversations had been comfortable. Tonight, though, it would be different as they would be meeting again face-to-face.

Already, butterflies of anticipation flitted in her belly at the idea of their gazes connecting again, though their date was still hours away. So why, then, couldn't she resist the temptation to glance at the police scanner, obscured by her bedside clock?

No, she wouldn't listen today. She'd promised herself for the last week that she would stop. The habit wasn't a healthy one; she knew that. She'd be humiliated if Brett realized her secret. What would she do if after he found out, he decided she couldn't accept his life? Brett was an honorable man. Would he decide that the honorable thing to do would be to walk away from her to shield her from her fears? Misery covered her, pulling down on her like a lead blanket at just the thought of it.

The scanner needed to go into the garbage. The little machine was only hurting her, the morbidity of its cryptic messages tempting her at her neediest level. She couldn't let that happen anymore.

She no longer believed Brett was marching into a gunfight every time he pulled his car out of the Brighton Post lot. Reality had turned out to be duller than the TV dramas she'd imagined. Brett was just as likely ticketing a motorist for careless driving or getting dirty while helping a stranded driver change a tire as he was having to draw his weapon. She knew that.

The only reason she still listened at all was to make sure that everything was okay in their general area. She even knew, courtesy of Brett, that the state police's eight-hundred-megahertz radio system operated on a frequency that could no longer be picked up on a scanner. So she only listened to Emergency Medical Service and fire department frequencies, anyway. Still, the long drone of the machine's tone gave her peace somehow.

Her gaze fell on the scanner again. She took a deep breath. She didn't need to listen. Didn't need the safety net that the sound provided. Then, defeat sinking into her spirit, she flipped it on.

"You should wear the black dress, Mommy."

Tricia jerked her head to see Lani propped in the middle of her bed, having carefully pushed two of the outfits out of the way. When had she come into the room? How could Tricia have missed seeing or hearing her?

Because the scanner chose that moment to beep, Tricia reached a hand behind her to shut it off.

"What black dress, honey?" She gestured with her hand toward the four outfits on the bed, not a dress among them and certainly not a black one. "What do you think of this outfit?" She held the sweater and skirt in front of her, swishing the skirt back and forth in front of her flannel pajama bottoms. Lani might have been an old soul in a child's body, but Tricia knew her daughter's weakness for a good swishy skirt.

But the girl only made a face and shook her head. "That's a church dress."

Tricia spread that outfit across the bed again. "What's wrong with that?"

"You need to be pretty for your date."

Tricia chuckled. "I'll do my best."

"Where are you going to eat?"

"At a special place, Five Lakes Grill."

Lani scrambled off the bed and rushed to the closet, pulling a plastic bag-covered garment out from the very back. "Wear the black dress."

Tricia was already shaking her head before Lani had wrangled the department store bag off a simple dress—yes, black—with a square neckline that was surrounded by a dusting of sequins. It was a lovely dress, appropriate for a special dinner out, and yet it was all wrong.

"Is it still new?"

"Yes." Tricia lowered her gaze to the bottom of the short sleeve, where tags, a few years old, were still attached. The red lines were beginning to fade where all of the markdowns had made it possible for her to own a dress like that. The one she'd purchased for an anniversary dinner that never happened. She'd worn a different black dress instead.

Lani stepped to Tricia and stretched to hold the dress up to her. "Are you going to wear it?"

Tricia ran her fingers along the seam of the lovely, never-worn garment. What was she saving it for? She closed her arms around the dress and held it to her. Symbolic, perhaps, but she was ready to get on with her wardrobe and her life. "Yes, I'm wearing it."

Max zoomed into the room. "They're here. They're here."

Tricia wrapped a robe around her and followed behind them to the living room. Already, Rusty, Jr. stood at the door with Rick and Charity.

"Hurry up, guys," the older boy called out.

"Thanks so much for taking them today," Tricia said as Rick stepped over to kiss her on the cheek. "This is a real treat."

"What are friends for if not to take your children hiking for the day?" Charity said.

Charity's knowing smile made Tricia wonder if her feelings for Brett were so transparent that just anyone could see them. But her friend was probably just pleased she'd set up a couple who actually liked each other.

"Come on, kids. Let's go." Rick grabbed Max around the waist and hauled him under his arm. "We've got a picnic lunch in the car."

That was all it took. Three children and two adults were almost immediately out the front door.

Tricia returned to her room and lifted the black dress off the bed, holding it to her in front of the full-length mirror. She gave in to the temptation to swish it in front of her.

It was so strange to feel this giddy anticipation, that same kind she used to know before she'd experienced life's broken promises. She couldn't wait to see Brett. Would he kiss her hello? Would he like the dress?

Well, she had a lot of day to get through before any of that could happen. Leaving the bag on the dress, she hung its hanger through the handle on the bureau drawer. On top of the dresser, she arranged her undergarments, a matched set of earrings and a necklace.

Those things would have to wait until later. Right now she had laundry to do and a shower to take. After returning her collection of outfits to the closet, she pulled the hamper over from the corner and began sorting clothes. Just to provide background noise while she worked, she flipped the scanner back on.

The piercing beep startled her. Her fingers had closed over the volume control when the machine blurted out, "State police requesting EMS. Send a med flight. Officer down."

The phone rang four times before it switched to voice mail just as it had each of the twenty times Tricia had dialed Brett's cell phone number in the last two hours. This time instead of just hanging up, she slammed her own phone receiver on the kitchen counter.

"Answer the phone, will you," she yelled, not caring how loud. "Brett, where are you?"

Pacing, she stopped in front of the television, where cryptic news reports had been interrupting regular programming for a least an hour. *State trooper shot. Condition unknown. Gunman at large.*

"No new details are available, but we'll be following the story this afternoon," said a pert brunette who might as well have been reporting about construction tie-ups on M-59 for the little compassion she displayed. The reporter stood there doing a remote from some rural location near the Oakland County-Livingston County border, answering no questions and appearing not to care if she did.

Tricia couldn't breathe as she sank onto the couch,

her blood freezing in her veins. Why couldn't they just say who'd been shot? Or how he or she was? But who was she kidding? The only thing that mattered to her was if Brett was okay. Selfish, awful person that she was, she wanted it to be someone else's husband or father or sister undergoing surgery right now. A person who someone else loved who might die today.

She shook her head. No, she couldn't be that cruel. She just wanted Brett to be all right.

Images crowded her mind before she could stop them. Reverend Bob and Rick McKinley at the front door with grim faces. A metallic blue casket. A granite headstone. Only this time, she imagined the state police at her door. But that nightmare was all wrong. No one would come to her to tell her. They weren't even married. No one would know how much she loved Brett, how her heart would die with him.

Unbidden, one of her recent conversations with Brett filtered through her thoughts. Delivering death messages, he'd told her, was the hardest part of his job, the part that gave him a sick feeling inside. "You try to be professional, but—you know what—I'm still a human being," he'd said.

Would another trooper be approaching his duty of informing Brett's parents with dread today? Brett hadn't even had his chance to make peace with them though he was trying. He couldn't die yet.

Dead. No, she wouldn't let herself believe it. There had to be some plausible explanation why she couldn't reach him on the same day a state trooper had been shot. Brett and that trooper weren't one in the same.

Lord, please let Brett be okay. Don't let him be taken from me.

A gasp of hopelessness caught in her throat. *Not again. Not again.* Because she wasn't ready to trust what she'd just asked God to do, she turned back to the television. Already the all-smiles reporter had vanished, replaced by Saturday sports coverage.

With shaking fingers, she dialed Brett's cell phone number again. He usually answered right away. And his private phone was as much a part of his regular equipment as the police radio and laptop. But now the phone rang once…twice…three times…four, then it clicked over to voice mail.

"Hey, this is Brett," his greeting said. "Leave me a message and I'll get back."

Could he get back? Or had that whisper of a kiss she'd placed on his lips been her unwitting kiss goodbye?

Tricia buried her face in her hands, tears escaping through her fingers. Had all her fears come true a second time? No, it couldn't happen.

But what if it had?

She'd been forced to do it before, to bury a man she loved. She'd had no choice but to get up each day, to breathe in and out and to feed, clothe and hug her children. All that she would have to continue, no matter what it took. But she could promise no more. The first time the lacerations in her heart had healed to rough scars. This time, she was convinced, the wounds were so deep, so profound, that she couldn't survive.

Brett wiped his hands on the slacks of his best suit and climbed out of the car. Okay, this day hadn't turned out as perfect as he'd hoped, but he wouldn't let a bad day destroy his great plans for tonight.

Too bad he couldn't prevent his stomach from rolling with thoughts of his shift, which included one of every trooper's nightmares. The reality that he hadn't starred in this bad dream didn't make any difference to the sick sensation that made him want to crawl out of his skin.

His steps slowed, the intensity of this knock to his professional family stealing his courage. When his foot reached the bottom step, he gave in and stopped. The curtain didn't move, but he still wondered if the children were behind it, ready to pounce. On other days he would have welcomed that, but today he just needed a moment to catch his breath.

Maybe Joe was right. Maybe he was jumping the gun. Sure, Tricia had confessed she loved him, but she probably wasn't anywhere near ready to commit to doing that forever.

Was he even ready? *Stop.* He finally drew in that breath he so badly needed. Second thoughts that threatened fell away as he exhaled. Yes, he was ready to live his life, and he wanted that life to be with Tricia and the children. The Father had led him to her; he knew that now. And he was ready to be the man who loved her and supported her, every day and every night for the rest of his life.

He patted the ring box in his suit pocket and climbed the steps to knock on the door. Nothing. Not even the rumbling sounds of rambunctious children. Knocking again, he waited.

Something was wrong. It was five o'clock. He was right on time. He glanced to the driveway to check again, but he'd already noticed her station wagon there. Opening the screen door, he knocked hard on the steel front door. This time he heard movement inside. He almost relaxed until he heard another sound melding with the creaks of old floors and cheap furniture. Sobs.

He couldn't wait any longer. The door was unlocked so he turned the knob and pushed it open. Though it was still daylight, the darkness from the drawn curtains cast the room in shadow. The only light came from the television, though its volume was muted.

"Tricia? Kids? Where are you guys?"

Another feminine sob drew his gaze into the darkness. There, in the easy chair in the corner, he saw Tricia, curling herself into a tight ball, her knees tucked against her chest. As he flipped on the light switch, he glanced back and forth between the pajama-clad woman and the television, and he knew what she knew. Or at least what she'd thought she'd known.

He rushed to her and crouched in front of the chair, delaying his impulse to gather her into his arms. All that mattered was Tricia. But she only sat there, staring at one of the dark walls and rocking.

"Sweetheart, are you all right? Where are the kids?" Whether for his sake or hers, he didn't know, but he couldn't stop himself from reaching to her and resting his hands on her shoulders.

Either his touch or his words cut through her daze, and she barreled out of the chair and into his arms, knocking him from his haunches, his backside hitting the floor. She buried her face in his shoulder, dampening his suit with her tears. He held her as tightly as she was squeezing him, gently rocking for a few silent moments before he pulled his head away.

"Are the kids with Rick and Charity?" He waited for her nod before he continued. "Good. They're okay. And so…am I." He smiled up at her where she'd come to rest on his lap.

But she only leaped up, shaking her head furiously as she landed back in the easy chair. "But I thought…"

He reached to flip on the table lamp. "I think I know what you thought, but I'm fine."

"You didn't answer your phone…all day."

He reached into his suit pocket for it, at the last minute remembering he was carrying the ring box and not the phone. "The battery died. I forgot to charge it. I left it at home on the charger."

It was an unusual set of circumstances, but he could tell from her expression that she didn't see the humor in it. "I should have called. It never crossed my mind that you would think—"

"When you didn't answer, didn't return my messages…"

"I'm sorry about the phone, but I wasn't involved in the shooting. I was on the other side of the county when it happened. The trooper who was shot while serving an arrest warrant wasn't even from the Brighton Post. He's okay though. He's already out of surgery."

But she was still shaking her head, not listening. Finally, he rested his hands on her shoulders. "Listen to me. Please. It wasn't me."

"But it could have been." She shook her shoulders as if to cause his hands to fall away, but he held her firmly.

"It wasn't."

"Next time, it might be."

"It won't be." He started shaking his head, as much to convince her as to push away the dread that now rested heavily upon his own uncertainties. No matter how much he wanted, he couldn't guarantee that. No one could.

Tricia leaped from the chair and rushed past him down the hall. He followed her to her room but only stood in the doorway. At first, the feminine black dress that hung from the dresser caught his attention. Had she planned to wear that on this date that he already realized wouldn't happen? Then he heard the static and glanced over at Tricia who turned off the scanner.

Strange how quickly his hope for salvaging this situation disappeared. "Why do you have that?"

But Tricia only shook her head. "I can't do this, Brett. Look at me. Look at what I've been reduced to."

He did look. Her eyes were puffy. She still had on pajamas instead of the dress. She looked as if she'd gone into battle and lost. He *felt* as if he'd done the same.

She indicated with her hand toward the scanner. "This is what I do when you're at work. I listen, just to make sure you're okay." Reaching to the wall, she yanked the plug out and stuffed the machine in the waste basket. "I can't do it anymore." Then she paused, squeezing her eyes shut, before she opened them again. "I can't be with you."

"Tricia, please…" He didn't know what he was pleading for. He'd already lost, and yet he couldn't give up on her—or let her give up on him without a battle.

She shook her head again. "I want you to leave."

"No." He remained where he was in the doorway, but he crossed his arms. "I'll go, but I'm going to have my say first."

Her eyes widened for a few seconds, but she shrugged, appearing defeated, and lowered herself to sit on the bed.

"Rusty was a fool. Don't you see that?" It was the first time he'd ever referred to her husband by name, and it felt wrong to criticize him, but it was long past time for Tricia to hear this.

She sprung off the bed and rushed at him, her hands fisted. "How dare you say something like that about him? You didn't even know him."

Brett put up his hand to stop her before she reached him. "Well, I know this about him. He didn't even realize what he had. He was so fortunate to have you and the children to love. He should have recognized that he was the luckiest man in the world. But he didn't. Otherwise, he wouldn't have taken so many dumb chances."

Tricia shook her head. "You don't understand."

"Don't I?" He met her gaze steadily until she stared at the ground. "You nearly said it yourself. He took one irresponsible chance too many, and it got him killed."

Instead of defending her late husband again as he'd expected since it only multiplied his misery, she covered her face with her hands. Through her fingers, she asked in a muffled voice. "Why are you doing this?"

He needed her to understand, but was that any excuse for being cruel and defaming her dead husband? He didn't know. Nothing seemed clear right now except that his life without her was…empty.

He raised his hands wide in a plea for understanding. "I know you're scared. My life involves danger. But police work is not just a job to me. It defines me. It's who I am, what God wants me to be."

Her fists had softened, and everything inside him

demanded that he hold her and take all of her fears away. But he couldn't. What he had to say was too critical.

"I love you, Tricia. So much that sometimes it's just too intense, this need to protect you. But I can't pretend to be someone else, even for you. I wish I could."

She wore this unreadable expression, so he didn't know if he'd reached her or not. Just what had he expected? That she would run to him and tell him everything would be okay? It wouldn't. He doubted it ever would be again.

The way his eyes burned told him he had to get out of there, unless he wanted her to see him cry. He turned to go, but he couldn't help saying one more thing to her, no matter how choked it came out. "If it were me, it would be different. I would never take unnecessary chances because I only want to come home to you."

Chapter Sixteen

Tricia sat on her bed enclosed by the darkness she'd sought the moment Brett had walked out of the house. Why had she let him leave like that? Why had she let him go at all? Those were the questions for the hour. She didn't have an answer for them.

She buried her face in her hands, tears escaping through her fingers. What had she done? Brett was gone. She'd thought he was dead, convinced herself to her core that it was true. And then to her amazement, he'd shown up unscathed. But she couldn't welcome him with joy, pulling him to her heart forever. All she'd been able to see was the next time, or the time after that. When her nightmares would become her reality.

So to protect herself from a heartbreak she couldn't survive, she'd sent him away. Some might have appreciated the irony in the situation, but it only compounded Tricia's misery. She'd so feared losing Brett to the risks he took that she'd lost him to her fears instead.

Tricia wiped away a few stray tears, figuring she had no right to cry them. She'd brought all of this upon herself by refusing to open herself to the possibilities. This world offered no guarantees. She knew that as well as anybody. But God did provide second chances to the undeserving every day. Brett had been hers. A chance at a new life. And now she'd lost him.

The ringing telephone startled her, and she pounced on it, hoping against hope. "Brett?"

"Tricia, it's Charity." She paused for several seconds. "Brett…um…called us. We're packing up our stuff, and we'll be over soon."

For several seconds, Tricia could only hear cell phone static. None of what Charity said made sense. Brett had called her? How had he gotten Charity's cell phone number to call while they were picnicking? And why was Brett still trying to make sure she was okay, even after she'd pushed him away?

But the answer was obvious. He really did love her, even when it hurt him to keep doing it. Even when she didn't trust him enough to love him back fully. Brett had been right about Rusty, too. He'd been right about a lot of things—including that she was scared. Terrified. But he kept right on loving her…and hoping.

"Tricia, are you still there?"

"Yes, I'm here."

"Do you want us to keep the children for a while longer? We can even keep them overnight if you want."

Tricia opened her mouth to refuse the offer. She shouldn't get in the habit of relying too much on her friends again. She needed to be independent, to provide for her family's needs all on her own.

Why? a voice inside her demanded. Why did she have to be some pillar of strength when someone loved her enough to share the load? *I would never take unnecessary chances because I only want to come home to you.* His promise sounded so tempting, a safe place to land when it felt as if she'd been falling for years.

Would she ever finally be ready to let go of the past and take a chance herself? A chance on love?

"Tricia?"

"I'm here, Charity. It's not necessary for them to spend the night, but would you mind keeping them for a few more hours?"

While she awaited her friend's answer, Tricia tucked the phone under her ear and moved to the closet, grabbing a pair of jeans and sneakers. From her bureau, she collected a sweatshirt and the rest of her clothing.

"Are you sure you should be alone? Brett said you were pretty upset."

Tricia yanked the shirt over her head. "I'm fine, really. There's just something important I need to do."

* * *

Tricia drew her jacket tighter around her shoulders as she continued past several rows of flat grave markers, a wrapped bouquet of daisies tucked under her arm. Dozens of times in the last two years, she'd found private comfort at Rusty's grave site. That her first love wasn't really there, but instead was enjoying eternity, had never prevented the place from giving her peace.

Until today.

She doubted anything could remove the uncertainty she felt inside, or the hurt, or the regret.

Crouching by that spot of earth with Rusty's marker at its head, she pulled a few weeds to tidy the site and then sat next to it, curling her legs under her. A breeze caught her hair, blowing it across her face, so she tucked it behind her ears.

"Boy, I sure messed up this time," she said to the piece of ground and her husband as she pictured him in Heaven. "Oh, Rusty, I just don't know what I'm doing. I love Brett, but I guess you already know that. He's a good man, like you…yet different."

She couldn't bring herself to say it aloud, even if Rusty wasn't really there to hear. She couldn't tell him that she loved Brett in a way she'd never been able to love him—as someone she could rely on, place her trust in.

If she could, then why hadn't she? Why hadn't she trusted Brett enough to place her whole heart and her hope in his hands? And a bigger question, was she ready to do that now?

A prayer formed deep inside her soul, gathering momentum until it frothed over in a plea for guidance. *Father, I feel Your leading here. I need Your strength to help me to trust…without fear. I don't want to be afraid anymore. Please show me how to live again. Amen.*

Finally, the respite she'd often found in this place was hers again. She breathed deeply because she could. Her lips pulled up into a smile because they could.

Glancing down beside her, she caught sight of the flowers she'd purchased for Rusty's grave, still wrapped in green florist paper. She carefully unfolded the paper and lifted the flowers out, preparing to insert them into the permanent vase on the marker. Again, the wind rose, this time catching the flowers and sending a few petals dancing on the breeze. Tricia watched the daisy petals floating away, as if they had no cares, no worries. Again she remembered the Scripture that spoke of the lovely way God adorned the lilies. She and Brett had discussed that verse on the wonderful afternoon they'd spent together—the day she'd begun to fall in love with him.

For several minutes, she stared down at the flowers in her hands, their appearance so pure, their fragrance sweet. Then she pulled out two flowers, both with multiple blooms, and settled them in the vase. Of the remaining flowers, she chose one, cradling it in her palm. With her free hand, she gently tugged a white petal loose and released it into the wind.

The action was so simple, and yet so freeing, that she released another. And another. She grabbed another flower and continued until only foliage remained piled on the crumpled green paper.

So many feelings were tied to those tiny white petals. Of offering her fears up to God. Of giving the past a precious goodbye kiss. Of walking with faith into a future without guarantees.

After all of the petals had weaved their way past other grave markers beyond the bank of trees, Tricia gathered the stems and returned to her car.

Misgivings returned the moment she slipped the key in the ignition. Yes, she was ready to step into a future with Brett, but had she already burned that bridge beyond recognition? No, she refused to believe that. He loved her just as she loved him. He would forgive her. At least she hoped he would. And somehow she had to convince him that she could accept him just the way he was—on and off the job. She had to convince him to give her a second chance. It was the biggest risk of her life, and she was ready to take it.

Having spent most of the weekend forcing himself not to phone Tricia, wrestling with his futile need for her, Brett was relieved during his Monday shift to finally be back on patrol. At least he had some control here, knew what was required of him and had the skills to meet those expectations.

With Tricia, he didn't have any idea. Why did his heart still long for her when her lack of faith in him had left it raw? His weakness was intolerable, clashing with the strength and certainty he expected of himself in his life and work. He prayed again for the strength to let her go.

At the beep on his laptop computer, he glanced at the new e-mail message.

Lunch at post on me. Meet in 20?

Joe

Brett turned the car around, making the quick return journey from Parishfield. A meal on Joe?

But when he pulled into the post lot minutes later, he was surprised to see so many cars and figured it was gun-permit day again. If not for the free food, he might have pulled right back out on patrol. Still, Halley's Comet passed by about as frequently as Joe Rossetti offered to foot the bill, so Brett wasn't missing this opportunity.

As expected, the building resonated with the sound of too many voices in the waiting room. At least he wouldn't have to face all those potential gun owners the way everyone in the radio room would since it was at the front of the building and the squad room was in the rear. Joe didn't appear to have made it back yet, so Brett took a seat at a computer terminal and typed in a report for a property damage accident at the beginning of his shift.

Ten minutes later, Joe came rolling past him, but

from the waiting room and not from the parking lot as he'd expected. Not only that, he was empty-handed.

"Hey, pal, where's the chow? Couldn't you find anybody who was 5-0 friendly?" he said, joking about the eating establishments that regularly give police officers a fifty-percent discount. It figured that his tight-fisted pal would bail on the plan when he had to pay full price.

"Something like that." But Joe's smile wasn't apologetic.

"You got me here. I expect to be fed."

"Is your stomach all you think about?"

"No." As if he'd even thought about food in the last two days when he hadn't been able to blink without seeing something that reminded him of Tricia.

"Well, if you want to get what's important to you, you're going to have to go out front."

Brett drew his eyebrows together. "In that mess?"

Joe nodded.

He shrugged and followed his fellow trooper out into the cramped waiting area. Then he saw the crowd. It was as if someone had transplanted half of the Hickory Ridge church congregation to the Brighton Post. In the center of all that chaos stood Tricia and her children.

Though he was accustomed to handling unusual situations with calm professionalism, this one he wasn't ready to take. Did he have to share his humiliation with the whole church community and all of his co-workers?

"It's Trooper Lancaster," somebody called out.

"Hey, Brett," somebody else chimed.

Brett glanced over his shoulder and caught Joe's conspiratorial grin. For a practical joke, it didn't begin to be funny. He turned back to the crowd and raised his hand to stop the flurry of activity. Already, he was taking a step backward for his retreat.

Tricia only stepped forward. "Brett, wait."

He shook his head. "I don't know why you're doing this, but it's not—" What? Fair? Right? Funny?

"Not as special as your elaborate proposal plan?" She flashed a nervous smile and gripped her hands together. "I know. I'm sorry. I didn't know where to hire a horse and carriage."

She wasn't making any sense. He figured Charity had told her about his plan to propose, but this was something else. "Tricia, what are you doing?"

"Don't you get it? I'm taking a risk."

His breath caught as realization settled over him in a fine mist. Emotion clogged his throat, making him wait before he could trust himself to speak. But he couldn't wait. He had to know right now whether the hope sprouting in his heart had any chance of surviving. Instead of speaking, he grabbed her hand and nodded toward the secretary in the radio room who buzzed them past the locked door into the back.

"Where're you guys going? We're all friends here." That time the voice obviously belonged to Rick McKinley.

Collective chuckles drifted through the open front

desk area as Brett led Tricia to the conference room where they could be alone. Before he'd questioned his ability to speak, but now he couldn't stop the words from spilling over.

"I need to know what you're saying." Somehow he managed not to say something overly dramatic such as what was left of his heart depended on it.

Facing him and grasping both of his hands in hers, Tricia stared into his eyes. "I'm saying I'm ready. I want to be the risk-taker this time…by giving you my heart. All of it."

She was saying what he wanted to hear so much that his chest ached with yearning, but he couldn't accept the gift when it came at her expense. "What about the scanner? I can't make you do this, Tricia. Every day you spend with me, you'll be waiting for the other shoe to drop. You can't live like that." He carefully slipped his hands away from hers and cleared his throat, the agony of what he was about to say re-opening wounds that he doubted ever would heal. "And I can't let you do it."

Tricia's eyes shone, and she rolled her lips inward in a futile attempt to stop the tears that spilled over her lower lids. He wanted to say anything, do anything, to dry her tears. Because he couldn't, he shoved his frustrated hands into his pockets.

"It's too late, isn't it?" She buried her face in her hands as if she already had her answer.

He opened his mouth to speak though he couldn't imagine what he would say.

But Tricia shook her head to delay him. "It took me a long time to get here. Too long. But I'm here. With God's help, I finally let go of my fears."

Hope betrayed him again, but he couldn't let it. "You can't guarantee the fears won't return, won't sneak up on you and send you right back to flipping on the scanner or listening for sirens or waiting for a knock at the door."

"No, I can't guarantee I'll never be afraid again, but I know now I can turn my fears over to God." She breathed out a burst of air that must been an attempted chuckle. "I've also made an appointment for pastoral counseling with Andrew Westin. I won't let my fears control me anymore."

"Oh." He knew it sounded ridiculous, but his mind was racing so quickly that he couldn't come up with a response. What was a man to say when the thing he wanted most in the world appeared within his grasp, and yet he wasn't sure he should reach out to take it?

"Brett, please forgive me. I let you take all the chances with us, and I didn't take any. I always kept one foot firmly planted in the neutral zone, so I could stay safe." She shook her head. "I don't want to be safe anymore. I want to be with you. I *love* you."

Yearning and uncertainty collided inside of him with the yearning pushing his own fears aside as he reached out to her and rested his hands on her shoulders. "You don't need to be forgiven. Being with me is a risk. Are you sure you can do this?"

But Tricia only met his gaze steadily, certainty in

her eyes where tears had been. "There's no greater risk than being without you. Than not having you to love for the rest of my life."

Because no words had been invented yet to express the enormity of the feelings bombarding him, Brett did only as his heart demanded and gathered the woman he loved into his arms. His kisses offered all the promises of his heart. Of permanence. Of hope. Of joy.

When he finally pulled his mouth away and rested his forehead against hers, his breath came in quick gasps and his heart strummed in his chest. Tricia's eyes had taken on a glazed look. On her lips, she wore a smile. He smiled back, glad that the one-way window next to them looked *out* into the interview room instead of vice versa.

"Everyone is waiting for us," he said finally. "What were you planning to do with all those people waiting out there?"

"They're all here to watch me propose to you."

He chuckled. "Well then, shouldn't we get back out there to them?" He waited for her nod before he added. "You go on ahead. I'll be right out."

After she continued down the hall to the waiting area, Brett made quick work of obtaining the prize from his locker and then jogged up to the front of the building.

"Go for it, Tricia," Hannah called out with a whoop.

"Here, Brett, sit." Andrew Westin indicated a folding chair they'd set in the middle of the crowded room, while the ad hoc choir broke out into a passable chorus of an old love song.

But Brett only signaled for them to stop. "No, Tricia. Why don't you sit?"

He took her hand and led her to the chair, dropping on one knee in front of her. Several "aws" filtered through the room, with cheers of glee erupting from the junior section.

They were surrounded by twenty people, not including the secretaries, sergeant and even the post commander watching from the radio room, but at this moment it felt only like the two of them. He pulled the felt-covered box from his pocket and held the simple ring out to her.

It was so easy for him to speak aloud the certainty of his heart. "I love you, Tricia. In a way I didn't know I could love anybody. I can think of nothing better than to share every day with you—and with Max and Lani and Rusty, Jr. Please be my wife and be the answer to all of my prayers."

Tricia's smile was enough to take his breath away. "You're the answer to my prayers, too. Yes, I'll marry you."

He slipped the ring on her finger and held her precious face between his hands a few seconds before drawing her to him for a tender kiss. He pressed his lips to hers once more as cheers erupted from their audience.

They were both laughing by the time they pulled

their heads away. He took her hand to help her stand. Together. Where they belonged.

Brett gestured toward their personal choir. "You brought these people to serenade us, right? Are they going to sing now?"

He waited, but as they started to sing, he turned to his future bride and lifted an eyebrow. He would hardly call The Byrds's classic, "Turn! Turn! Turn! (To Everything There Is A Season)" a love song. But then he figured songwriter Pete Seeger hadn't planned on this butchering rendition when he'd adapted the lyrics from the Bible, either.

"Ecclesiastes? I was expecting a love song."

Tricia skimmed a hand down the side of his face as though he was precious. "It is a love song. Our song. Remember? 'A time to kill, and a time to heal; a time to break down, and a time to build up...'"

She paused and stood on her tiptoes, touching her lips to his in silent promise before lowering again. "And, Brett, this is a time for us."

Epilogue

Tricia stood before her bureau mirror, removing the hairpins securing the simple ivory veil that matched so perfectly with the tea-length summer bridal gown. She couldn't help running her hands down the smooth silk skirt once more though she doubted she would ever forget its softness. Already, everything about this day was emblazoned on her memory—their promises before God, their indecently long kiss and the many smooches with the children that followed.

Still, the day was far from over, even though the children were probably already bedded down at Rick and Charity's house where they would be staying a few days. Here in the house where she'd lived another life, another precious moment was yet to come today, and butterflies crowded her tummy with sweet anticipation and misgivings.

"You are so beautiful. How did I get so lucky?"

Startled, she turned to see Brett leaning against the door frame as if he'd been there for a while.

She fussed with the remaining hairpins to give her hands something to do. "I didn't know you were there."

"I know. I just love watching you."

They had that in common. All day she hadn't been able to take her eyes off him, so handsome in his black tuxedo, the amber specks in his light brown eyes appearing to sparkle more than usual today. Already he'd removed his jacket and bow tie and rolled the sleeves of his tuxedo shirt.

"I should have known better than to get married in July," he said, wiping a drip of perspiration from his brow. "But then I didn't want to wait until fall, either."

The smile he turned on her sent the butterflies inside her fluttering again. She breathed deeply to calm herself, but his masculine scent only filtered through her nostrils. The scent of her husband. Her friend. Clasping her brush in her hand, she nervously drew it through her hair.

Instead of remaining by the door, Brett crossed the room and lifted the brush from her hand. "May I?"

Brett was surprised to see his hand tremble as he drew the brush through the silky brown tresses. Having recognized her nervousness, he'd only wanted to calm her. So who was going to help remove his anxiety?

But as he watched, the face of the woman whose

reflection he shared in the mirror turned up into a lovely smile. A trusting smile.

"It was a beautiful ceremony, wasn't it?" she said, her voice sounding wistful.

Breaking the promise he'd made himself not to bring up the past, he asked, "As pretty as the first one?"

"This one was ours," she said, closing the subject and promising him a future without comparisons in the same simple response.

"It was nice, wasn't it?" Because it was calling to him, he drew a long tress of her hair to his face and inhaled its clean scent before brushing it against his lips.

She jerked slightly as her breath caught, took the brush back and finished the job. "My parents really like you."

He slid his fingers through her hair, tucking it behind her left ear. That left open a long expanse of her lovely neck that he was powerless but to honor with his kiss. "I'm glad, but it only matters what you think."

"I think you'll make a great husband."

"That's because I have a great wife." Speaking that last word aloud for the first time since the ceremony, he felt a jolt of joy inside. God had given him more blessings than any one person deserved. Absently, he pressed his lips to her neck a second time, smiling when he felt her pulse racing. Something told him their private moments would always be this way, filled with sweet honor and delight.

"My mom and dad are thrilled you picked me," he said, trying for levity, though even he could hear the thick emotion in his voice.

"I picked you? Wasn't it the other way around?"

"Was it?"

Their gazes connected for several long seconds in the mirror. But then he grinned and shrugged. "They're finally coming around, you know. Especially since I told them you only went out with me because you were so impressed that I was a cop."

Her eyes widened. "You told them that!"

"I did." He rested his hands on her shoulders, and she sank back against him, perhaps symbolically placing herself in his arms.

"So when are you going to tell them the real story?"

With his face buried in the satin of her hair, he shrugged. "I will eventually. I figure we have plenty of time for that story. And even about a blind date where I got stood up."

They both laughed at that, but as Brett wrapped his arms around her middle and drew her closer to him, their laughter fell away.

His next words were so filled with love that they came out as only a whisper. "But even my parents have to see that God had a plan for us."

Again, she held his gaze in the mirror. "Yes, He did."

At that admission, he turned Tricia, and she came willingly into his arms. As he touched his lips to his wife's, he thanked the Father for this precious gift. He gathered Tricia to him, feeling complete and wonderfully blessed. Tonight they would express their love to each other in private moments, joining hands and hearts as they started building a new life together.

*   *   *   *   *

If you enjoyed A NEW LIFE,
you'll love Dana's story in next
month's Christmas Anthology,
A FAMILY FOR CHRISTMAS
"Child in a Manger,"
available November 2004.
Don't miss it!

Dear Reader,

Does God offer only one perfect love in a lifetime,
or does He give us the hope of finding it again?
I explored this question and my belief that the Father
provides us with second chances at love as I wrote
Tricia Williams's story. The young widow believes
she's already known lifetime love, so she doesn't see
the possibilities in Brett Lancaster, the state police
trooper who just might be able to help her to overcome
her fears and heal her heart.

In writing *A New Life,* I had the opportunity to
visit with the people of the fictional Hickory Ridge
Community Church for a third time. I have enjoyed
living with these characters and watching them
grow in their lives and in their faith community.
I hope you have enjoyed getting to know them, as
well. I love hearing from readers. Please feel welcome
to contact me through the following Web sites:
www.SteepleHill.com or www.loveinspiredauthors.com.

Dana Corbit

Take 2 inspirational love stories FREE!

PLUS get a FREE surprise gift!

Mail to Steeple Hill Reader Service™

In U.S.
3010 Walden Ave.
P.O. Box 1867
Buffalo, NY 14240-1867

In Canada
P.O. Box 609
Fort Erie, Ontario
L2A 5X3

YES! Please send me 2 free Love Inspired® novels and my free surprise gift. After receiving them, if I don't wish to receive anymore, I can return the shipping statement marked cancel. If I don't cancel, I will receive 4 brand-new novels every month, before they're available in stores! Bill me at the low price of $4.24 each in the U.S. and $4.74 each in Canada, plus 25¢ shipping and handling and applicable sales tax, if any*. That's the complete price and a savings of over 10% off the cover prices—quite a bargain! I understand that accepting the books and gift places me under no obligation ever to buy any books. I can always return a shipment and cancel at any time. Even if I never buy another book from Steeple Hill, the 2 free books and the surprise gift are mine to keep forever.

113 IDN DZ9M
313 IDN DZ9N

Name	(PLEASE PRINT)	
Address	Apt. No.	
City	State/Prov.	Zip/Postal Code

Not valid to current Love Inspired® subscribers.

Want to try two free books from another series?
Call 1-800-873-8635 or visit www.morefreebooks.com.

Love Inspired®

Steeple Hill's exciting
FAITH ON THE LINE
series continues with...

PETER'S RETURN

BY

CYNTHIA COOKE

Protecting the cover he'd
painstakingly constructed over
the years was not as important
to Peter Vance as rescuing his ex.
Dr. Emily Armstrong had been
kidnapped because Baltasar Escalante needed her specialized
care for his dying son. Yet once the drug lord learned a trap had
been set for him, Peter and Emily found themselves on the run
in the Venezuelan countryside. Would Peter be able to save his
former wife from Escalante's wrath...and could he and Emily
redeem the past?

FAITH ON THE LINE: Two powerful families wage war
on evil...and find love

Don't miss
PETER'S RETURN
On sale November 2004

Available at your favorite retail outlet.

www.SteepleHill.com   LIPRCCPOP

Love Inspired®

A DRY CREEK CHRISTMAS

BY

JANET TRONSTAD

She was not a thief! But Brad Parker refused to believe
Millie Corwin's explanation for why she'd been in Dry Creek's
café when he'd found her. What kind of person snuck into a
place to leave presents for people? Once he got to know Millie,
he realized she was as lovely on the inside as on the outside.
Yet she was indeed responsible for a crime:
stealing Brad's love-resistant heart!

Don't miss

A DRY CREEK CHRISTMAS
On sale November 2004

Available at your favorite retail outlet.